A GOOD SOLDIER

To Bob,
Thanks for
coming by
tonight!

JEFFREY MARKS

An Imprint of The Overmountain Press
JOHNSON CITY, TENNESSEE

This book is a work of fiction. All names, characters, places, and events are either the product of the author's imagination or are used fictitiously. Certain historical references are factually represented to the best of the author's recollection and research. Any other resemblance to actual events or persons, living or dead, is entirely coincidental and beyond the intent of either the author or the publisher.

Hardcover ISBN 1-57072-215-3
Trade Paper ISBN 1-57072-216-1

Printed in the United States of America

1 2 3 4 5 6 7 8 9 0

To Rob, Robyn, and Spenser

Money is a good soldier, sir, and will on.

Merry Wives of Windsor, Act 2, Scene II

ACKNOWLEDGMENTS

I'd like to thank Rob Schofield and his mother for their help in pointing out Civil War inconsistencies. Rob Perry is my best friend for more than his invaluable assistance in editing and suggestions, but those never hurt.

Of course, it goes without saying that the people at Overmountain and Silver Dagger have been extraordinary. Beth Wright is a wonder to work with, and Sherry Lewis is an editor from Heaven. Karin O'Brien is an incredible publicist for them, and she should take a bow for all her hard work.

Matt Kovach gets a special mention for letting me read his Civil War ancestor's diary that included a number of battles which Grant participated in. It made for many nights of fascinating reading.

My parents, of course, besides giving me the opportunity to write, have helped immensely with Grant lore and local sites. Beyond the Butler County Library in Batavia, Ohio, and their historical society, a number of research books came from my parents' collection of Southern Ohio history. In reading about the final days of the Confederacy, I was amazed to learn of the lost Confederate gold. While it's now been 137 years since the end of the war, there's still no conclusive explanation for what happened to over $40,000 in gold and silver.

The Civil War Museum in Philadelphia, Pennsylvania, gets a special mention for their wonderful collection of biographies and artifacts from the era that made me step back into the 19th century for a day or two.

These people have provided me their knowledge; any mistakes are my own.

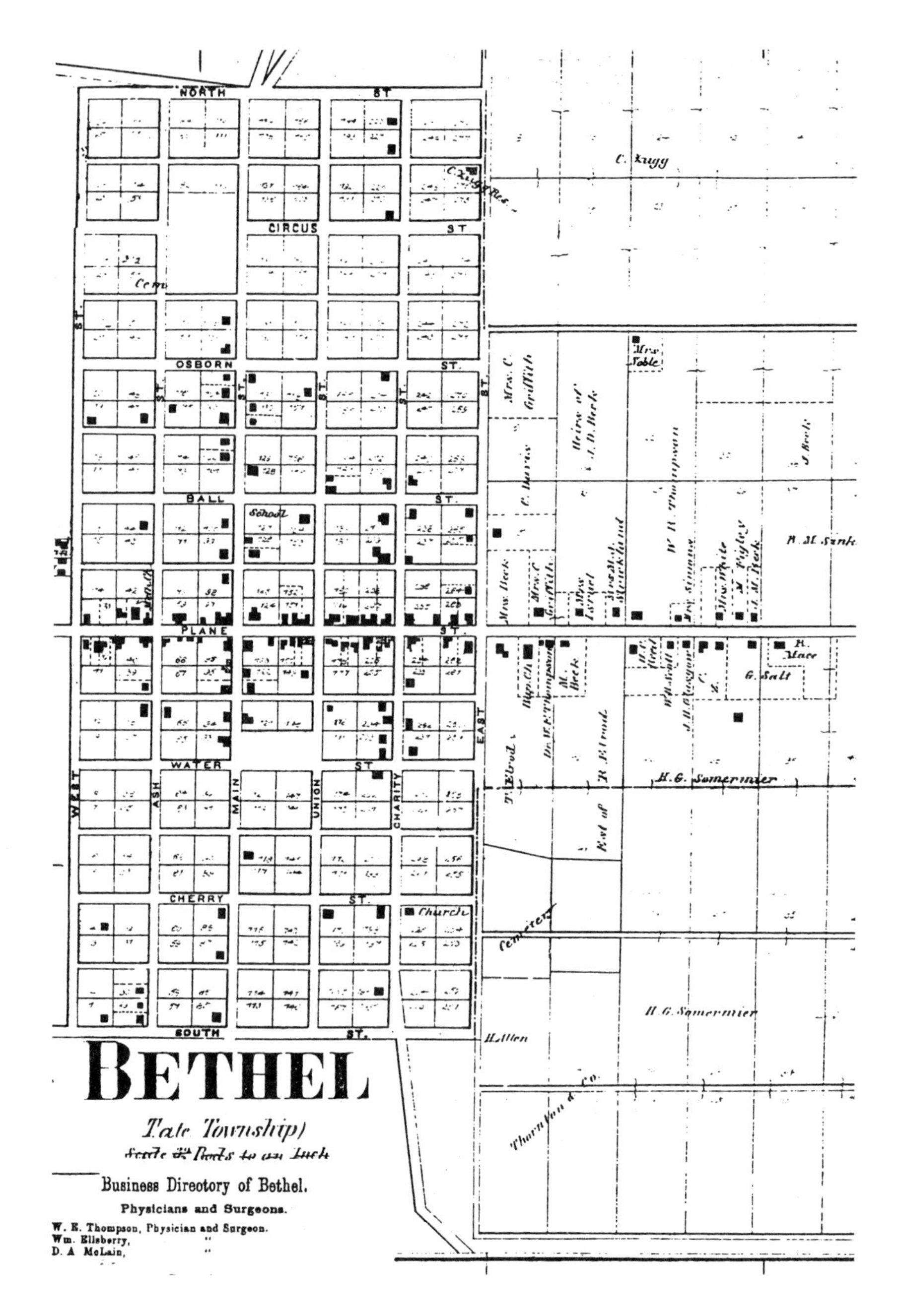

Bethel, Ohio, as it appeared in 1865, from Atlas of Clermont County, Ohio, *by Lube and Gordon, published in 1891.*

INTRODUCTION

I've learned the hard way that a historical mystery takes months of research to get the details right. Ulysses and Julia Grant did take the trip recorded in this book in September and October of 1865. Some of the stories used in the novel are true. I did take creative license by reversing the Grants' trip from Cincinnati to Georgetown.

While the town of Bethel resembled what is portrayed in the book, the people in the novel are fictional except for Grant and his family. All the other characters are my creations.

I grew up in the shadow of Grant by virtue of my birthplace. Many of the stories about Grant I've known for years. It only made sense to write those down as part of this novel.

CHAPTER · 1

ULYSSES S. GRANT recognized death as he paused at the home's entrance. The black crepe that clung to the door had swaddled the coach light in its doleful clothes. This family was in mourning. He hesitated to intrude. Yet at the same time, he and his family had accepted an invitation to make this their home while staying in Bethel, Ohio, for a few days. The village of a few hundred souls was barely big enough for a tavern, much less a suitable hotel.

His wife, Julia, and little Jess, their son, waited in the carriage. His father, Jesse Root Grant, had already left to seek out his old cronies for lodgings. Grant could imagine the older man, chest puffed out till the fancy, gold-braided buttons on his jacket strained against their threads, telling his friends about how his son had whooped the Rebs single-handedly. How any of the Bethelites could manage to house the man's big ways was beyond Grant.

The tiny town lay halfway between Cincinnati and Georgetown on the coach route. Ohio was dotted with tiny farm communities like the place that he'd visited during his summers off from West Point. Grant had grown up in Georgetown, and shortly after he had left for the military institute, Jesse uprooted the family and moved to Bethel.

One of many such moves to improve the family's station, it was more than likely made, Grant thought, so Jesse could find a fresh batch of people who hadn't suffered his strong opinions. The prosperous tanner had found the smaller community more to his liking. He had even been the first mayor of Bethel after it incorporated in 1851—a fact he mentioned with every breath when talk of Grant's rumored presidential nomination arose—and called his mayoral election a landslide, as if thirty-one votes could be a majority of anything.

Grant had visited the village as much as the Army allowed, and Julia had stayed in Bethel during two of her pregnancies and had given birth to their second son, Buck, in the tiny town, followed by Nell, their only daughter. Although Fred, their oldest, and Jess, their youngest, were both born in St. Louis, Bethel held a tender spot in his heart as the birthplace of his offspring.

Now Grant stood in front of one of the finer homes in Bethel and wasn't sure what his welcome would be. The dark fabric that shrouded the hurricane light by the door fluttered in the wind. He hadn't seen Chris Halley in nearly a decade. He'd been looking forward to recollecting about the old days. Back then, Grant had thought himself unfit for military service. So much for his prognostications.

That seemed so long ago. His friends had not been quite so war weary. He'd heard about Halley's capture during the war and his imprisonment at Andersonville. The mere word made Grant shiver like someone had plunged a bayonet into his grave. The prisoner-of-war camp had been the scourge of the South's efforts to defeat the Federals.

While Southern leaders sat on their hands, over 10,000 men died of disease and starvation in the overcrowded prison camp. Grant didn't know the precise number of men lost in Andersonville, but he'd fought campaigns with fewer casualties. So much for Bobby Lee's airs of a genteel Southern army man. His treatment of the slaves and prisoners of war made a more telling story than chivalry and fancy dress uniforms. The South had needed every captured man exchanged to continue fighting, and Grant had suspended prisoner trades. The stories which filtered back were unbelievable. The worse the conditions got at Andersonville, the more pressure was put on Lincoln to give in to the Rebels.

The inhumane conditions were still being discussed in Washington. The camp commander—that coward Captain Henry Wirz, who was a foreigner, to boot—was on trial for war crimes for his treatment of men like Halley.

How ironic it would be for Halley to survive his imprisonment and then expire just a few months after returning home. Andersonville had taken a toll on the prisoners' constitutions. More inmates had been wasted by disease and dysentery than by guns and knives. Grant shook his head and faced the door again. Here he was, all maudlin, and he didn't even know the facts.

Grant raised his hand and rapped on the door. The noise echoed inside the house. As he turned to return to the carriage, the door opened a hand's width. A woman lurked behind the wooden structure.

She stood five feet tall—if that—and was dressed from head to toe in the deepest shade of black. Her dress was new, bombazine or grenadine or one of those dull fabrics he knew from Julia's shopping. Dark black crepe covered the lower half of the skirt, reminding Grant of the door's decoration. A thick mesh veil covered her expression, except for the occasional sniff.

Grant couldn't be sure if this was Mrs. Halley or one of her children. The little ones had a way of getting big while you were off fighting wars. Two of his own sons, Fred and Buck, were nearly grown. Nell favored her ma, which left only little Jess to make him feel like a pa.

The woman raised her head to look at him, then gasped. "General Grant, forgive me. I'd forgotten about your arrival. . . ." Her words drifted off into the late September breeze. She opened the door farther and laid a gloved hand on the general's wool jacket. The autumn day was sunny but still cool enough to warrant his outer garments.

Grant cleared his throat and looked at her. "I'm sorry about your—"

The woman stopped him and tilted her veiled head up at him, but he couldn't tell a thing about her expression through the thick material. "It was Christopher. He passed away suddenly last week."

Grant nodded and tried to signal a look to Julia. She would know what to say, how to handle a widow woman. She was the more experienced in social graces and awkward situations.

"It was rather sudden. We weren't expecting it at all." The woman paused and followed Grant's gaze. "Oh my, forgive me. I forgot all about your family." She retreated beyond the doorframe.

Grant studied his dusty boots. "Perhaps we should stay elsewhere so as to not impose on you in your time of grief. John Young is still in town."

The woman shook her head. "You must not have heard. John was killed in a skirmish at the end of the war. One of the graybacks guarding him at Andersonville shot him squarely in the face." Despite the harshness of the message, the woman didn't seem to have any shivers in speaking it. Perhaps the war had hardened them all.

Grant tried to take in the notion. Two of his possums from younger days dead. How many like them had he seen on the battlefields? Bodies stacked three and four deep, so high that you couldn't see the ground. The country had paid a high price to see unity again, including Mr. Lincoln's death. Grant had to believe that a single nation was worth the sacrifice.

He still pondered his next step. He couldn't very well impose on a grieving family, but at the same time, Bethel was not the kind of town where lodging would be easy to come by. If Young and Halley were dead, that didn't leave many options. He'd be content to sleep on the ground, but Julia would have a conniption. Only five men had been his companions during his summers in town. Now two were gone.

He started to turn to look at Julia, but a large man on crutches joined the woman at the door and caught his attention.

"Captain Sam, I thought that was you." The man offered a hand out from the crutch. "What are you doing here?"

Grant could see him more clearly now and spied the familiar pants leg pinned above the knee. The man was dressed in a black suit with a white shirt whose sleeves showed the signs of wear against the crutches. His dark hair was streaked with gray, slicked back for the occasion. Muttonchop whiskers covered the start of jowls.

Grant squinted to recognize the man but kept coming back to the missing leg. None of his chums had been injured, or so he thought. Even so, the man knew his West Point nickname, a sobriquet that few remembered. Only Sherman, a few men from Bethel, and old classmates still referred to him as Sam.

"It's Zeke Newman. You remember?" The hand stretched out a bit farther, and the general clasped it in both of his hands.

"Zeke, sure enough." Grant marveled at the changes and wondered if he, too, had changed as much. It had been over a score of years since they'd last seen each other, and the man barely resembled the lad he'd known. At least one comrade had survived.

"That your wife and boy out there? Here, have them in." Newman managed a few steps out onto the porch and waved a hand at the carriage.

Grant wondered how long ago his friend had been injured. The war was full of men who'd lost an arm or a leg to the cause. The most common cure for gunshot wounds was amputation.

"You'll be staying with me, Sam. No arguments. The widow Halley isn't in any shape for company. Let me tell the driver where to take all your luggage."

Grant's shoulders relaxed. At least he'd be able to spend the night in Bethel and not have to travel on to Cincinnati. He wasn't up for the thirty-five-mile trip after spending a full day with his father and family. He needed respite. A nice hot bath and a good cornhusk mattress might do the trick. He smiled, thinking how soft he'd gotten since the war.

Julia stepped down from the carriage, giving a hand to little Jess. The boy bounded from the sideboard and barely escaped the mud along the street's curb. He galloped up the stairs and threw his arms around Grant's left leg, a luxury Newman could never afford.

The troop followed Newman into the house. The casket of their late friend reposed on the dining room table. Even in the half-light of the oil lamps on the walls, the box was hard to miss, an elaborate affair of fruitwood and brass. A coffin plate in the form of a small shield had been attached to the head of the casket. CHRISTOPHER HALLEY, BELOVED HUSBAND, FATHER, AND FRIEND. A GOOD SOLDIER TO THE END. The dates of his too-short life were etched into the metal. Grant thought he could still see shavings from the engraved numbers.

As ornate as the casket was, Grant couldn't take his notice from the body inside. He would never have recognized the cadaver as his friend. The chubby boy was gone, replaced by a rail-thin man. The dark suit was miles of fabric too big, and his hands were so frail that Grant swore he could count bones. Halley's sunken-in face showed his cheekbones in high relief.

The state of the corpse fascinated him. Grant was used to the natural decomposition of men, the bodies he'd seen in battle that had quickly been reduced to bones and rags. The hot humid days of Mississippi and Tennessee had seen to that. Halley was a different matter altogether.

The man had been embalmed, drained of blood and filled with chemicals. Grant gave a small shiver to think of the abuse the man's lifeless shell had endured, all to look a bit better before giving way to dust. Such artifice, not to mention expense.

While the family had always had a right bit of money, he knew that the Halleys didn't have as much as his own father. Jesse would rather burn his greenbacks than see them poured into the veins of a dead man to be preserved like a taxidermist's model. Grant knew that they'd done the same thing to Lincoln for his long trip back to Springfield, but that was the President being viewed by thousands, not a soldier in Bethel, Ohio.

Halley's body made him more aware of his surroundings. The gargantuan mirror which hung on the opposite wall only accentuated the opulence of the room. The table was a thick cherry wood surrounded by chairs that looked like they could have been Hepplewhite. Grant knew the furniture artisans from the stately homes he'd captured during the war. The homes had been the finest that the South had to offer, and now he found the same décor in a Bethel farmhouse.

He could discern the same appraising glance in Julia's gaze. She ran her eye across the tender porcelain dishes and the silver flatware. Even Julia's family, the haughty Dents, at their beloved White Haven couldn't do any better than this. She was probably lamenting the death of Halley from a standpoint of not being able to bask in such lavish surroundings.

Newman seemed to pick up on the home's surprises. "We used to talk about death a lot—back when we were down South. Halley always said that he wanted to be buried up right proper if we didn't end up in a shallow, numbered grave there.

It was the least we could do for him when his time came."

Grant nodded. The soldiers he'd known had jawed about the same thing. They'd written letters to their loved ones before battle, afeared that they would never walk off the field. Dying was a necessary part of war. The letters were not only a farewell to their kin, but identification as well. Those soldiers planned in advance for the possibility of not living to another nightfall. They knew the risks but chose to fight for their country.

He wasn't sure how the men in Andersonville stood the uncertain conditions. Grant wondered if you could live with death on that scale and come out the same man. They were trapped inside those log walls without clean water, living on cornhusks and raw meat, like livestock. They hadn't enlisted for penal servitude, even if it helped save the Union. A heavy price to pay for patriotism. How did a country thank men for what they had sacrificed?

Money would be no good in replacing a person. Grant wasn't really comfortable with the idea of paying a death fee to the families. The questions of a man's worth were hard to answer. Was a captain worth more than a private? How much was a limb worth? Or two limbs?

People tried to put a price on serving in the Army. Early in the war, wealthy men had paid boys to take their sons' places in battle. Grant shook his head. Nothing more than indentured servitude with a gun. The rich always tried to keep a cushion of cash between themselves and reality. If a rich person could get a body to die in his place, he'd manage it somehow, Grant was sure.

Little Jess interrupted his thoughts, making more noise than a tribe of red men. He whooped down the hall after the Halley brood. Children seemed inured to death, fast forgetting the deceased and the pain of loss. Grant marveled at their resilience. He hoped the country could heal as quickly.

Newman laughed at the sight of the children. "I think we might better be getting home. I'm sure you're tuckered out after that trip."

Nodding, Julia gave the man a half smile and went to collect Jess, while Grant murmured a few words of condolence to Mrs. Halley.

The widow seemed not to notice that the group was leaving. She looked out the window without acknowledging Grant's words or Newman's good-byes.

The group went slowly down the porch stairs and across Plane Street, the main east-west street through town. The coaches and carriages which passed through Bethel had rutted the path. Most people knew of the town only as a stop on their travels between Cincinnati and Georgetown. Grant smiled, thinking how the world had almost passed this place by.

Jess practically galloped circles around Newman as they made their way down the street. The boy certainly was wound up over something. Perhaps the travel or spending time with his father after so many years in battle. Grant wished for a fraction of the lad's vim.

They reached their destination, only a few houses away, and Newman opened the door to another good-sized home. Grant was surprised, to say the least. He had expected a more modest dwelling. The Newmans had never been moneyed. They'd owned a shanty—two bedrooms for six people—on the skirts of the village. And now with one leg, he could afford a two-story in Bethel. Grant had to wonder at the marvels of this little hamlet. Social caste didn't seem to mean anything here. Perhaps the war had produced a liberating effect on Bethel's citizens. Or maybe folks had decided to honor their veterans for service, like Philadelphia and New York had done for him.

Julia paused at the door, letting her husband and son enter first. Newman stood in the entryway and pointed to the stairs, cocking his head in the same direction. "Sorry if I don't go up with you, but these confounded walking sticks don't see eye to eye with them stairs. If you need anything, give Patsy a holler. She's the help."

Newman limped off into the darkness beyond the entryway. Grant eyed the staircase of curved dark wood railings and carpeted steps. After the long, bumpy carriage ride from Georgetown, it looked like a path to heaven. Julia took little Jess by the hand and mounted the stairs with resignation. Grant followed behind her, lugging two of the carpetbags they had brought along. The trunks could wait until later.

The room at the top of the staircase was large enough to house three generations of Grants. A huge bed staked the center of the room, circled by a fainting sofa and three wooden chairs. The room was heated by a small fire, which licked its logs in the hearth. Grant deposited the luggage near the fireplace and made his way to the bed. He pulled out the trundle for Jess and found it already prepared with sheets and pillows.

He turned to find a speechless Julia looking at their son. There were times when he found that his wife was less than firm with the children. From her struck expression, this might be one of those moments.

He marched over to the pair and inspected them more closely. Jess had taken his coat off and stood in a dirty white shirt. Surely Julia had seen worse garments from their three untidy sons. The boy's shoes were dumped on the floor, but it was natural to want to run barefoot in the likes of Bethel. Not many people in this part of the country had the wherewithal to buy shoes.

Julia held out her hand to Grant. Even in the dim light of the fire, he saw three coins. From what he could tell, they looked gold. Each coin had an eagle with outstretched wings on it, making a majestic flock of birds in her hand. Double eagles.

The fire's light sparked a golden glow on the coins, as if they were winking at the trio. But the gold couldn't be real. The three $20 coins added up to several months' wages.

"Wherever did you get this?" Grant thought of all the hard times when $60 would have saved him from the ignoble fate of selling firewood on a St. Louis street corner or borrowing from his father.

His jaw just about hit China when, before Julia could answer, Jess spoke up. "Papa, those boys gave it to me. They said it was play, not real." The boy looked like he might cry. His bottom lip stuck out as far as it could go, and the corners of his mouth trembled.

Julia looked at her husband. "Ulys, I'm speechless."

Grant tried not to chuckle, now knowing what it took to silence his wife. He rolled one of the coins in his hand. He twirled it in his fingers and tried to take a bite. Solid as a bullet. Anything could be play money, but from the look and feel of the coin, he was pretty certain these were real gold pieces.

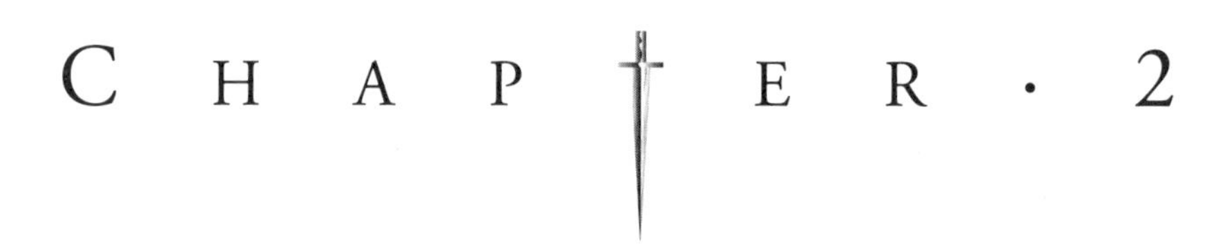

CHAPTER · 2

THE DAWN CAME with the musty gray tone that seemed to last from late September to March in the Ohio Valley. The blues and grays reminded Grant of the colors he'd seen the previous four years. An opaque mist hung from the tops of the trees and muted the fall hues. *Perfect day for a funeral,* Grant thought as he pushed his face into the pillow and wished for more sleep.

Their room at Newman's had been gracious. The mattress was thick and comfortable. Grant had had no trouble in falling asleep serenaded by the rhythmic breathing of his wife and child. He hadn't woken until the thick aroma of coffee filled his nose. He'd grown accustomed to chicory and root brews during the final battles of Virginia. Supplies of real beans were just too much extra cargo, and he had his men forage for what they could find. Coffee had been a luxury then, and the mere scent of it now filled his lungs with joy.

Julia must have smelled it as well. She slipped out of bed quietly and started her morning ablutions. Jess didn't stir during the splash of water or rustle of clothes from the carpetbags. Grant then followed her without waking their son. He was amazed at how soundly the boy slept, especially if the lad knew what his mother had in store for him.

The couple had stayed up talking after putting Jess to bed, discussing what to do with the money. Julia had been all in favor of marching their son back to the Halley house immediately, but Grant's calmer words had prevailed. He'd encouraged her to wait until dawn, believing that the widow and her brood would be beat after the viewing. The funeral was set for morning, and tradition always took people back to the house afterwards. Neighbors would call with vittles, and the family would find the kitchen stocked with enough food to feed them through the early days of mourning.

Grant had pocketed the coins and decided to talk to the widow after the funeral. The coins would be safe until then, and the family wouldn't likely be looking for the hard currency any time soon.

Jess awoke and Julia shooed him off to the outhouse, giving the Grants a moment alone. She rested on the edge of the bed, trying not to crease her best black dress. "Ulys, I can't bear to think of Jess involved in thievery. There just has to be an explanation."

Grant nodded. "I hope there is, but we'll find out soon enough. I expect the children were playing or something. But we need to give it back."

She nodded. Julia had known the Halley family better than he had. Her time in Bethel during her pregnancies had earned her some friends in the town. Grant knew her to be remiss in correspondence—Julia could be the worst epistle writer—so he didn't know how much she had kept up with the townsfolk since her stays in the 1850s.

How much of the Halleys' funds did this money represent? With a husband in a prisoner camp during the war, Mrs. Halley couldn't have much to her name. The long battle for unity had made paupers of too many ordinary folk.

Jess bolted up the stairs, looking almost presentable. Julia managed to bring his collar to attention, and the family descended the stairs to find their host.

Drinking the coffee that had woke Grant earlier, Newman sat at the dining room table, a large mahogany affair. He had dressed for the occasion in a full-length black dress coat and tie. A black hat sat on the chair next to him.

Grant knew that funerals fell just behind weddings as serious social engagements in the villages of Southern Ohio. The events were spread out over multiple days, starting with the laying out of the body, followed by the visitation, and then the funeral itself. Once the body was interred, the eating began. Grant saw two pies on the table in front of Newman and figured they were from his wife, whom they had yet to greet.

"Well, Captain Sam. You clean up right nice." Newman's face broke into a grin at the sight of his old friend. "Can't say that I've seen you look this good."

Grant cracked a half smile on his lips. He felt a mite guilty for enjoying himself at a time when Halley was dead and waiting to be buried, but he had looked forward to this trip for a dog's age.

Being called "Sam" again brought back a flood of memories about a happy time in his life. He marveled how a simple man could end up with so many names. When he went off to West Point, the government, in its infinite wisdom, had decided that his name was "Ulysses S. Grant," not "Hiram Ulysses Grant." In order to accept his appointment at West Point, he had to don a new name. Everyone knew that the government couldn't have made a mistake, though Grant often suspected that the real root cause rested with his patron, Congressman Thomas Hamer.

The initials "U. S." stood well at a patriotic institution like the Academy. He'd been "Uncle Sam," then "Captain Sam," and then later just plain "Sam." Even Julia, who had met him through his Point roommate, called him Ulysses or Ulys.

"Well, I haven't had much cause for fancy," Grant replied. "There doesn't seem like much point when the Rebs are firing on you." He didn't like dressing up for the military, though many of his commanders did. They could sport the fancy dress uniforms, but he'd managed to wear results instead. Grant had modeled himself on his informal leader from the Mexican War, Zachary Taylor. He'd hesitated to pull out his finery in Bethel. He recalled an early trip to the town in his full West Point regalia. A little boy with red stripes painted on his trousers had followed Grant around. The whole town had mocked the general's hubris after that.

Newman opened his breast pocket and pulled out two cheroots. He proffered one to his guest and took the other for himself. Grant immediately recognized the full scent of local tobacco. Probably Newman had grown the plants on his farm.

"Sam, I got a favor to ask of ya." Newman struck a match on the edge of the dark wood table and inhaled sharply as he pressed the flame to the end of the cigar. Thick gray puffs of smoke nearly obscured his face.

"What's that?" Grant looked for a suitable surface to strike his match. Julia would die if she saw him scuffing good furniture, especially for something she considered to be a filthy habit. He finally lifted one foot and struck the match on the sole of his boot. Grant savored the flavor. He'd picked up the cigar habit after he'd left Ohio, so the taste of the local tobacco was still a unique joy. He enjoyed the moment, knowing that Julia would be back in a few minutes and insist on putting it out.

"I have to go somewhere after the funeral. I was wondering if you could stop back here for the pies and take them to the widow Halley for me. I'd be much obliged."

Grant nodded slowly. Small price to pay for his friend's hospitality. "I'd be happy to, but wouldn't your wife want to take them herself? I don't want to steal any thunder from her cooking."

Newman turned his head as he blew out a plume of smoke. "Theda died two winters ago. I got the news when I was at Belle Island. She was carrying a child for us. Neither one of them made it. The pies were made by the colored help." He grunted as he stood up and found his crutches. He slid one under each arm and made his way for the door.

Julia and Jess still waited in the parlor as Grant and Newman left through the front door. The tiny procession followed Newman outside and down the path to the dirt road. They all turned left and walked along Plane Street to the cemetery.

Grant could see people in the distance, congregating in the cemetery. Despite the misty disposition of the day, the men had removed their hats as a sign of respect, and the women's heads were bowed. He guessed that it had to be for Halley. The village wasn't big enough to need multiple funerals in one day. The gravedigger's death from overexertion would be next if that were true.

A score or more people gathered at the grave. All eyes shifted to the strangers. Grant got a couple of grins from those he recognized, but no one made a sound, out of respect for the dead. The preacher, or at least the man at the funeral who was carrying a leather-bound Bible, nodded and looked to Mrs. Halley. She began to weep as the man cleared his throat and read from the book:

"To every thing there is a season, and a time to every purpose under the heaven: A time to be born, and a time to die." The preacher looked around the group for a reaction, then continued, "A time to plant, and a time to pluck up that which is planted; A time to kill, and a time to heal; a time to break down, and a time to build up."

Grant searched the crowd for familiar faces but found few.

He saw a man who might have been Adam Woerner, but he couldn't be sure. No sign of the Browns at all. He recognized Mrs. Halley, her face shrouded by a veil.

She was steadied by the comfort of a young boy who couldn't have been more than ten. Grant looked at him, standing as tall as his mother. The lad would have a hard life trying to earn a living for the family after his father's death. That chore fell to the oldest when a parent died.

One person Grant had no trouble recognizing came over and threw his arm around the general as if he hadn't seen him in years, rather than a day. In a knee-length overcoat with polished gold buttons and his affected gold-rimmed glasses, Grant's father looked every bit the prosperous merchant that he was.

Jesse Root Grant had moved from abandoned child to tanner to merchant to mayor of Bethel. Still, he managed to rankle people wherever he went. A vehement zealot against slavery, he'd actually worked for John Brown's father at one time.

Jesse was in his element in Bethel. The farmers and townspeople treated him like an old friend and royalty. With his expensive clothes and gold trim, he didn't let them forget it either. He'd moved from Bethel years ago, but he'd made a special trip from Covington to help his son bask in the glow of notoriety. At a rally in Georgetown, he'd managed to talk for nearly ninety minutes after the general's three-minute speech.

Now Grant hoped that his father wouldn't try to steal the thunder from the deceased. Jesse had made a career of turning others' events into his own opportunities.

The preacher finished the readings and managed a few words about Halley. Despite the pats and hugs from loved ones, the widow broke down twice during the ceremony. Grant looked at his own wife and couldn't imagine life without her. He'd endured too much time away from Julia during their marriage. He planned on making the most of his leisure time. If the powerbrokers were right, Andy Johnson would be a one-term president, and Grant himself would be the next commander-in-chief. Even in the White House, he and Julia wouldn't be able to enjoy time alone. Too many people traipsed through the Executive Mansion, looking for jobs and favors.

How far removed from his life his friends from Bethel seemed now. He'd risen through the ranks during the war to its highest echelons, and his five friends had lingered in Andersonville for over a year. Grant had met Lincoln; these men had seen comrades starve to death. How much different could their paths have been? Yet at one point, they'd all ridden the hills of Southern Ohio together, spent time at the same swimming hole. Who knew what turns life had for you?

Grant wondered if there were any hard feelings. Did they look at him and see what they could have been? The men didn't seem to harbor a grudge. Newman and Halley had welcomed his family into their homes. That didn't speak of bitterness from the war.

Grant turned his attention back to the preacher. The parson had about finished extolling Christopher Halley's virtues. For all the death he had seen, Grant had not experienced many funerals in the previous four years. Corpses of men not afforded a proper Christian burial had littered the battlefields. Those who had managed to be interred were put into common graves with their fallen comrades. The army was usually on the move by the time the dead were laid to rest. Lincoln's funeral was one of the most recent ones he could remember—as well as one of the most painful.

Mrs. Halley threw a handful of dirt onto the casket and turned away. She retreated towards the black iron gate.

The soldiers who attended started into their routine. Shoulder arms, present arms, shoulder arms, rest. Attention, shoulder arms, load at will, and fire. Grant knew those proceedings all too well.

After the guns were quiet, the rest of the mourners took their cues from Mrs. Halley and fell in behind her. A few of the group stopped to talk to her as they started back to her house. Grant took the opportunity to approach her. Julia nodded as she took little Jess by the hand and reluctantly followed her father-in-law to the widow's house.

Grant cleared his throat and looked down at the ground. He wished he had a nice veil to hide his discomfort. He didn't need to see her eyes and the grief that they would clearly show. "Mrs. Halley, I hate to bother you in such a painful moment, but I have the most embarrassing of things to relate."

She looked up. "What might that be, General?"

He held out the three gold coins in his palm. The eagles nearly flew in formation, and he pushed his hand towards her. "My son took these last night by accident. You have my most sincere apologies."

She looked toward his eyes and brought a hand to the area around her mouth. He wished that Julia were still by his side to interpret womanly gestures to him. He had never understood the fairer sex. "Thank you for your kindness, General. I appreciate your generosity, but our family will be fine. Your charity isn't needed. Christopher provided well for us in death."

"But, ma'am. These were taken from your house." Grant felt his cheeks burn in the cool autumn air.

"Most kind sir, we have no gold in our house. I'm not sure where your son received the coins, but they do not belong to my family." She turned and started off to her house and the guests who had come to bid her husband farewell.

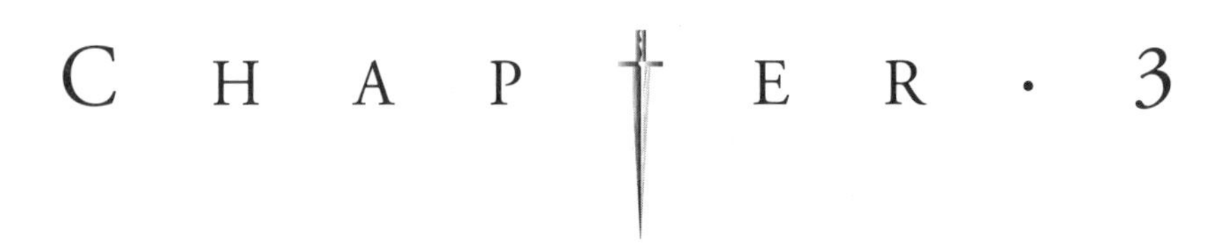

JULIA KNITTED HER BROWS, and her one good eye looked at Grant with suspicion. "Of course Jess took the coins from her house. He said so. He's not a liar, Ulys. I know my son."

"But, Mama, they gave me the coins," the boy protested beside the couple. They had come to the widow's home.

Grant needed to consult his wife on what had just happened. He couldn't believe that Mrs. Halley was lying. Still, he'd impressed the importance of the truth on his offspring. Jess, the carefree one of their brood, had never shown any signs of stealing before.

Julia pursed her lips into a thin line of disapproval that reminded Grant of his mother's expression. "Well, Mrs. Halley said differently, Jess. She said they weren't hers." Julia turned to her husband. "Perhaps they belonged to someone else who was there, Ulys." She tapped her demi-boot on the floor as she tried to think of an explanation.

Grant knew it was useless to try to interrupt her in one of these moods. She would puzzle something until she had an answer or wore herself out. Best just to stand back and let her have at it.

Jess flounced down on one of the chairs and crossed his arms over his chest. The little boy looked as if he might burst into tears. Grant was pretty sure that his son had no reason to lie about where the coins had come from. Jess had already been chastised for taking the money.

Grant looked behind him to the milling people in the next room. So far no one had come in to see why the Grants had taken to themselves. Perhaps it would be attributed to no more evil motive than big-city thinking—the notion that the general and his family were now too good for the likes of Bethel.

Jesse came into the room and harrumphed. He'd taken off his wide-brimmed hat to show a mane of wild hair. "What are you doing in here, son? You need to be out there, wooing voters."

"We're trying to solve a problem." Julia gave Jesse a withering glance that he didn't seem to notice. He lived in a world of his own making, one where right was decided by Jesse Grant and no others.

He looked at the coins Grant was holding. "Where on earth did you get those? I haven't seen any like that in years." He picked one up and flipped it over in his fingers, twirling it like a spin top. Grant knew that most merchants dealt in greenbacks now, rather than gold.

"We don't know. Jess says he got them here at widow Halley's place, and she says she's never seen them before. We were just discussing what to do with them." Grant watched his father treat the coin like an old friend.

Jesse handed the coin back to his grandson with a formal bow. "Well, if they don't belong to no one, then they must belong to you."

"That's not right." Julia snatched the coin from little Jess and stomped into the other room. As easily as she listened to her own father's poppycock, she had no tolerance for her father-in-law's mercenary ways. She considered her family to be old money, even though the money was no older than the debts amassed over the war years. Grant fully expected the Dents to be asking him for money in the near future, an ironic twist from the days when Major Dent had given him the land for Hardscrabble, the home Grant had built by hand.

He decided to follow her into the living room to make some small talk. He'd had enough worrying about money. If no one missed it, then there was no hurry in giving it back. He would indeed give it back, though.

As he scanned the room for Julia. He noticed Jess from the corner of his eye and hoped that the boy wouldn't accept any other presents from the Halley children. Grant's nerves couldn't stand any more kindness from the likes of them.

As he looked around, he observed a man standing next to Mrs. Halley. Grant still had trouble believing that his friend had passed away. Destiny seemed so fickle that two members of the squad from Bethel had been struck down like that. Yet he'd heard of whole families decimated by the war. There was no quota on lives in the pursuit of freedom.

The man handed the widow a small bag and turned to leave. The man's present reminded Grant that he'd forgotten the pies. He found Julia and quickly explained where he was going, then headed towards Newman's house.

The good thing about a small village like Bethel is that it takes only a few minutes to get anywhere. Grant took the stairs at double time and flipped open the door as he hit the top step.

No one bothers to lock a thing in towns like this, he thought. *They didn't see the thieving and looting that went on in war.* The general had occupied more than one stately home where the residents had tried to hide their valuables. The spoils of war went to the victors.

Grant didn't bother to knock. No one would be home except the colored help, from what Newman had said. He opened the front door and made for the dining room. The two pies still cooled on the table, where he'd seen them before the funeral.

Balancing one in each hand, Grant started back to the entry. He heard voices upstairs and stopped for a moment, surprised that anyone was home. Had Newman come home early, or was someone else on the second floor? Grant worried momentarily about his own possessions.

The voices were low, but he could still make out a few words of the conversation. It didn't sound like the voices of any colored Grant had known.

"Found the money."

Another voice that Grant didn't recognize mumbled a few words that sounded like acquiescence. The voices didn't get angry or yell. That would have made it easier to hear what was being said.

Grant shrugged and headed to the door. He almost collided with a petite freedwoman who was entering the same way. She stood barely five feet tall, thin as a spring sapling and dressed in a plain blue gingham dress. Her rail-like arms were heavy with vegetables and a gourd that threatened to overwhelm her. Her bushy gray hair was the only thing about her that didn't look small.

"Land sakes," she said, "you must be the general. Mr. Newman said we'd be having company. Let me get that for you." She held open the door for Grant to leave. "I'm Patsy. Mr. Newman hired me on to look after the place, after his wife passed."

"Thank you kindly, ma'am. It's nice to make your acquaintance." Grant started down the steps to the front walk. "I'm assuming these are your makings?"

She nodded at him. "Yes, I'm glad to see that you remembered them. What with Mr. Newman being gone and all. I was a mite worried that they'd be forgot."

Grant looked back at the house with its two stories and multiple windows. That was a lot of home for a man living alone. "Mr. Newman isn't gone. I thought I heard voices inside the house."

The old woman frowned and bunched up the wrinkles on her forehead. "That can't be. I saw Mr. Newman ride off a few hours back, and his mare is still gone. He never goes anywheres without that horse."

Grant could empathize with the man's desire to have his horse. Cincinnati, Grant's own steed, was stabled back in Washington. He missed the horse which had led him to so many victories for the Federals. They had felt comfortable together, nearly as compatible as he and Julia were, in their own way. Still, he was certain he'd heard his friend's voice in the house.

Grant wanted to look into the matter, to prove the woman wrong, but the weight of the pies was becoming a nuisance. He wanted to set them down, but that would mean retreating back into Newman's house for no good reason, instead of persevering on to deliver the pies to the Halley family.

He made his way through the gate without trouble, then started down the dirt road again. He passed a sole rider on Plane Street. Bethel was about as long and narrow as Patsy. It existed as a farming community and a stop for the stagecoach riders.

The street took a dip down by a creek and rose again near the Halleys' place. Grant saw his father's old house. Even though both parents had lived there, he always thought of the ostentatious home as his father's. No wonder. Jesse Grant was every bit as magniloquent as Hannah Simpson Grant was plain. Their home in Bethel had once belonged to Thomas Morris, a U.S. Senator and a member of the richest clan in town.

Now Grant's friends lived in homes that were as stately. He

had grown accustomed to his father's pretensions, but he had yet to figure fancy airs in the poor farming families he'd known growing up.

His mind stole back to the gold coins that Jess had found. If the boy was to be believed—and Grant knew him to be essentially honest—then one of the children had given him the coins. But how would the Halley children come upon that kind of money? Grant couldn't answer that question, but he wanted to, and soon. He didn't like having doubts about his youngest. The boy was near and dear to his heart. Jess brought a smile when few things could take his mind off weightier matters.

Grant went to the back of the house, where he deposited the pies on the counter with a dozen other desserts. A few of the womenfolk meandered about in pockets of gossip as he forded the crowd. Grant wanted to ask them about the Halleys' sudden wealth, but it would be ill mannered to do so here and now. They were to pay respects to the deceased, not try to determine how he'd made money.

Grant marveled at the home's opulence as he noted the chandelier in the entryway. For all his success at war, he'd failed at business. He'd been practically destitute when the war began. Four years of steady pay, and increases in rank, had set the family right again. Now with the war over, Grant couldn't believe the way the country treated him. The people of Philadelphia and New York had bought him homes. Other cities had given him cash, steeds, more than he could ever want.

Yet, not everyone had fared so well during the war. Halley had languished in a prison camp, so how had this family come into such money?

Grant made his way to the parlor, where Mrs. Halley sat shrouded in the black garments required for mourning. He had nearly greeted the widow, when his father took him by the arm and escorted him to the woman.

"Good evening, ma'am." Jesse bowed deeply from the waist like a play actor.

The widow merely nodded. Grant couldn't tell if it was politeness or frosty indifference brought on from his father's rather vivid past in Bethel.

Jesse adjusted his wire-rimmed glasses and peered down at the woman. "I just wanted to let you know how deeply sorry we are about Mr. Halley's passing. In fact, Ulysses and I made a donation to the church here, in the amount of three gold coins, as a token of our sympathy. We knew that the reverend would make good use of it."

The widow's eyes lit up. Grant could see them glow even through the black veil covering her face. "Thank you, Mr. Grant. That was most thoughtful of you."

Jesse took his son by the arm and led him to a cubbyhole off the main hallway. "There, son. I fixed that problem right up."

Grant tried to discern some clue from his father's face. "What exactly did you do?"

Jesse put his forefinger to his temple. "Just made a few deductions. I took it for granted that my namesake was telling me the truth. He got that money from this house. So for some reason, she didn't want us to know that she had a bunch of gold coins laying around. I didn't want Jess to sound dishonest, so I gave them to the church. Albeit, the clergy are a darned sight more greedy and dishonest than any Grant would ever lay claim to."

"So why tell the widow Halley?"

Jesse looked over his son's shoulders, trying to reconnoiter for anyone who might overhear them. Grant knew that if anyone overheard them talking, the word would be all over the village by the time he sat down for dinner. On the other hand, gossip cut both ways. Perhaps the townsfolk would know the origin of the gold pieces.

"She knows where those coins came from," Jesse whispered. "There's only so many ways for a woman to come by that much money in a town like this. And since she isn't telling, there's only one thing that we can do."

Grant cleared his throat. The thought of being in cahoots with his father on any proposition was daunting. The thought of joining forces with his father to protect the family's good name was more than he could take. "Since those people maligned my boy, we're going to get to the bottom of this mystery and find out where those coins came from."

CHAPTER · 4

GRANT WAS ABLE to stave off his father's indignant quest until the next morning, but just barely. Jesse was up at the crack of dawn in search of vindication for his grandson. He pointed to the steeple that marked the tallest structure in town. Not that Bethel had many contenders, but the Methodist church rose far and above the nearby homes, the Swing general store, the business of Sargent and Griffith, the McCall druggist, the Lloyd harness-maker, and the blacksmith. Since most of the homes lined Plane Street, the height was easy to measure.

"There might have been a war," Jesse said, "but things still operate the same in a small town. If you want to know something, go to church. I plan on following the money in this conundrum. You can't go wrong with that advice."

Grant looked at the church, the same one his mother had attended when she lived in town. He wasn't sure what to expect from the preacher, though his father seemed assured.

"You're about to see some of the positives of being a politician, son." Jesse adjusted his coat and brushed at a few specks of lint on the sleeve. "You'll get this treatment soon enough."

The front door to the church was unlocked, and Jesse strode inside. Grant followed. The building had tall, thin, stained-glass windows on each side. The light that entered sparkled with stripes and flashes of red, gold, and green. The pews looked like quilts of color.

Grant couldn't spy anyone in the sanctuary, but Jesse didn't hesitate, marching to the front of the building and up onto the dais. He leaned inside the door behind the pulpit and began speaking. Grant took his own time in making his way to the apse. By the time he reached his father, the old man had the parson hanging off every word.

"Reverend Evans, I don't know if you remember my son. This is General Ulysses S. Grant, my eldest." Jesse always referred to his son by his full name—despite the fact that it wasn't even his given Christian name—if there was something to be gained. He put a hand behind Grant and gave him a shove forward.

Evans nodded and smiled. "Of course I remember. It's been a long time though, General."

Grant tipped his hat and smiled. "Indeed it has, Reverend. How are you?"

"Just splendid. I'd heard word that you were in Bethel and thought I spied you at the burying yesterday."

Jesse rested his outstretched arm on the preacher's desk and placed three gold coins on the wood surface. Grant was sure that those were the coins little Jess had found, but when the old man had been talking with Mrs. Halley after the funeral, it sounded as if he'd already donated the funds.

"What is this for?" Evans glanced at Jesse, though his gaze crept back to the coins in a matter of seconds. Even hidden from the stained-glass windows, the little stack glittered. Grant knew that this much hard cash would buy a lot of stained glass.

"Mrs. Halley asked us to drop the money off," Jesse replied. "She's too distraught, but she wanted to express her gratitude for yesterday." He looked straight at the preacher without flinching. Grant wondered how his father could equivocate without showing it on his countenance. It must be six kinds of sin to lie to a man of God.

"It's just one of the duties I do to tend to my flock." The man had the good graces to redden at the thought of all that money. Lincoln's greenbacks were the legal tender, but nothing caught the imagination like gold.

"Oh, but sir, you know that the Halleys came into money. Some of it must go back to the One who made it possible."

Evans nodded quickly, his head bobbing up and down. "Well, the family made a rather sizable contribution when Brother Christopher returned from the war. They called it a donation of thanksgiving."

"This looks like the widow's mite, so to speak." Jesse didn't let on for a moment that he didn't have any notion about the source of all the money. If Grant didn't know any better, he would have thought that his father and the preacher shared equally in the knowledge.

Evans cleared his throat. The topic of cold hard cash seemed to make the man uncomfortable as he patted his brow with the forearm of his black jacket. The morning air was much too chilly for his perspiration. The frost had barely melted off the fields. "Well, I wouldn't go that far. The money was sizable, but our congregation has many needs. We've used the money prudently."

Jesse took a step back and placed a hand on his chest. Grant hadn't seen such acting off the stage in quite some time. "I had no doubt that it was," Jesse said. "I merely was commenting. Please, take no offense."

Evans slumped into the latticed-back desk chair. "None taken, Mr. Grant. I'd be happy to show you the books. Most of the money went to upgrading the steeple and the bell. We installed new pews and were able to buy seed this spring for three families who didn't have enough to get a proper crop started. All that, and we still had more than $300 left over. Very stewardlike, if I do say so."

"I agree. Prices just have not been the same since the war. Those greenbacks will ruin us yet." Jesse patted the stack of three coins like he would an errant child. Grant knew that his father lied. Even though many people still backed the gold standard, Jesse had made a fortune from the war. "We won't waste any more of your time, Reverend. Thank you so much." He bowed slightly at the waist and took his son by the arm to leave.

They had barely made it to the vestibule when Jesse began to cackle. He stopped and removed his glasses. He polished the right lens while Grant looked on. "I'm saying about $7,000."

Grant eyed his father—the man definitely had a nose for money—but he didn't see where this was leading. "What are you talking about?"

Jesse started on the left lens and tilted his head back towards the lantern above them. "Maybe more, but I can't see the good widow cheating on a tithe."

Grant leaned up against the doorframe and decided to wait. His father would tell the story at his own pace and in his own way. No use in getting perturbed or trying to hurry him. "So the money given to the church represented a tithe from the Halleys?"

Jesse nodded and adjusted his glasses behind his ears. "Yup, and based on what the reverend spent on construction and saved, I'm guessing it to be about $700, or a tithe from $7,000. So them boys came home with about $35,000, all told."

Grant stood up straight. He couldn't imagine that kind of money for soldiers, much less for prisoners of war. "How do you figure that?"

Jesse opened the door to the church and motioned his son through it. "Well, if those five boys were riding together, no way that one of them could find that kind of money without the others knowing about it. So I'm guessing that they all found this money and split it five ways. The widow Halley might be able to convince her husband to tithe for their part, but no way would he tithe for the whole group. So I'm guessing it's about thirty-five thousand, five times about seven. Or there 'bouts."

Grant stepped into the cool autumn sun. As they walked towards the church's front gate, a few scattered locust leaves swirled down Plane Street. "So those were Mrs. Halley's coins all along?"

Jesse nodded and scratched his beard. "Most assuredly. The woman lied about little Jess."

"There's something very wrong to blame a child for stealing and lying like that. What should we do now? Go see the sheriff?" Grant looked around at the small town, wondering if the law would be in the village buildings.

"Can't do that one. Sheriff Crosson lives out in Wayne Township, but it's no never mind to us. He's in Higginsport seeing about some new hogs. I took the liberty of asking the mayor about him when I stopped in for a visit."

"So, then, who can we talk to about the gold?"

Jesse gave him a sly grin. "Well, you're looking at the acting magistrate until the sheriff's return on Friday. The mayor didn't want to be involved in accusing the son of the leader of the Federal Army of thievery. Who better to leave it to than a family member?"

Grant remembered his father's magisterial duties from his stint as mayor of Bethel. Jesse had been asked to try a case involving ruffians shortly after he was installed in the position. As the trial progressed in the tannery, one lad had been so entranced by the details of the case that he forgot to watch himself and slid off his seat into a barrel of oil. Jesse had told the story for weeks to anyone who would listen.

Grant grunted and moved towards the street. "We have a reprieve then from any accusations. We both know that Jess wouldn't steal from anyone. So where would the Halleys get that kind of money?"

Jesse smiled and unlatched the gate. He looked both ways before stepping into the street, even though the road lay bare for as far as the eye could see. "Son, there aren't many ways for a man to get that sum of cash, especially after the war. It wasn't like they could hoard it for years. They were in a prison camp, of all places."

Grant nodded. The men would've had to have earned the money during the short few months since the end of the war. He'd received the spoils of victory from the country, but that was different. He'd been proclaimed a hero and the victor. These men had been trapped in Andersonville, a place that few in the North wanted to think about. Outside of the military and the men who had been there, many people didn't even know about the lethal prison camp in southwestern Georgia. Indifferent guards who paid no heed to the needs of the infirm had run Andersonville. As the wounds of the war began to heal, memories like those needed to be put behind the country. The Henry Wirz trial would end soon, and Grant had no doubt that the Butcher of Andersonville would be found guilty of war crimes.

Andersonville held no place for industry and wealth. Anyone with money would have bribed his way out of those plank walls. That meant the gold coins had come after the war, after the end of the fighting. That sum of cash was the wages of the gunrunners and blockade runners, not infantry.

Jesse started back to the Halleys' home. He had a purpose in his step that Grant recognized from his youth; he had a mission. "Son, I hate to tell you this about your friend, but there's only two ways to get that kind of cash. One is to steal it and the other is the government—which is just another method of thievery in most cases."

Grant frowned as he tried to keep step with his father, the same man who dragged his feet going to church socials. "Steal it?"

"There was a lot of anarchy in the South after the war. Train tracks were tore up, banks looted, and currency worthless. It would be an ideal time to pillage and not be caught. It could be years before someone makes heads or tails of the mess of their banking system, and even then who would know what had really happened to all that money?"

"I just can't see them stealing money." Grant shook his head. He couldn't believe that his possums would resort to thievery. The military should have taught them respect for institutions and authority.

Jesse cleared his throat and looked towards his son. "There is another explanation, but I don't know how you'll feel about hearing this tale out of me."

"What? I just don't see how they could have come across the money legally. It isn't possible."

"There's one place in the South that had plenty of gold—Richmond. Old Jeff Davis left town with a boxcar full of gold. Stories go that no one knows persactly what happened to it."

Grant sighed and shook his head. "Not rumors about lost Confederate gold. I can't tell you how many men I had to discipline just after the war for wasting time looking for that."

Jesse laughed. "Just like you, Ulysses, to think of a treasure in practical terms. The fact remains that no one has seen hide nor hair of that money since it left Richmond. My sources told me that it passed through Georgia. Maybe the Andersonville boys found it and helped themselves. After what they went through, I wouldn't blame them one iota."

Grant shrugged as he thought back to May, four months earlier. The end of the war had brought chaos to the South. The Confederate tender had been worthless. The price of gold wasn't much better. Davis had paid the troops who guarded him with some of the gold, but the temptation to take it all had to be great. Men with guns did as they pleased when order was lacking. The overriding fear of the Confederate government officials was that the Federals would be harsh in punishing the traitors. Some men had just gone home to wait. Jeff Davis had supposedly donned a dress to try to outwit his pursuers. Breckinridge and Butler had escaped to Cuba in tiny boats. In a situation like that, anything could have happened to the missing gold.

Grant's own troops had tried to locate the loot. Reported sightings of the money had ranged from Valdosta and Savannah to Lake Okeechobee in Florida. It was a lot of territory to cover at a time when troops were needed to battle Confederate skirmishes and a brewing crisis in Mexico. Still, the gold would be helpful in getting the country back on track fiscally. Old Salmon Chase had printed all those greenbacks without the gold to back them.

"I know the rumors," Grant said. "I heard all about them in Washington. The gold is gone. Jeff Davis's papers were buried somewhere. It's all out there. But you're telling me that five men from Bethel, Ohio, found the gold and brought it back here."

Jesse smiled. "Do you have a better explanation for what happened? I can't think of nary a one."

Grant looked at his father. No need to come up with another explanation now that Jesse had proposed this one. "I can't think of one, but it just can't be." The idea had become a termite, boring into his brain. Once inside, it only pushed deeper.

Jesse started walking down the road again. "Well, there's

one way to find out. We can ask them."

Grant stopped short. This trip with his father was going to drive him to drink. And sadly, Bethel had gone dry just after Jesse left the mayoral office. Grant frequently wondered about cause and effect. He mentally cursed that he couldn't have grown up in a larger city where a man could get lost and inebriated if he wanted. In small towns like Bethel, the shadow of his mother, Hannah, fell far.

"You're just going to march in and ask one of those men if they took the Confederate gold?"

Jesse shook his head and stepped up his pace. Grant's father was never more animated than when thinking about money. The thought of a fortune would likely make him frantic. "We're going to ask the widow. She's the one most likely to tell us what we need to know."

CHAPTER · 5

GRANT FELT ILL AT EASE inside the Halley house again. One of the boys, black armband around his tiny bicep, had answered the door, and Grant's heart broke trying to inquire after the lad's mother. Hadn't the family lost enough already without interference from him? He steeled himself thinking that if Mrs. Halley knew about the gold, then she had willingly thrown little Jess to the wolves of suspicion in allowing people to think he stole those coins. The thought of his son's good-natured face and easygoing disposition goaded him on.

For once, Jesse was silent; he allowed his son to do the talking. Grant knew that to the widow of a military man, the leader of the Federal Army would cut an imposing figure—even more so than the former mayor. Barring that, hc would make a plea to their friendship from years gone by.

Mrs. Halley stepped to the door. Grant couldn't read any expression on her face. The thick black veil covered her eyes. He knew that he used his beard in the same way, hiding emotions between the reddish brown tendrils. Had she intentionally donned the veil to mask her feelings?

"General, what a surprise. How can I help you?" Her voice was huskier than he remembered it. He assumed that her grief was real and taking its toll on her.

Grant bowed at the waist and concentrated on what he and Jesse had practiced on the way over. "Well, ma'am. I was hoping to talk to you for a few minutes. What with all the commotion around the funeral and all, I didn't feel like I got to pay my proper respects. Why, I don't even know how Christopher passed on."

The woman retreated. Her hands gripped themselves into fists. "For your information, Christopher did not pass on. He was murdered."

"Murdered?" It was Grant's turn to take a step back, and he nearly toppled backward down the stairs into his father. Jesse steadied him with a hand on his back.

The veil nodded. "Perhaps you should come inside, sir. We'd do best to not talk about this in front of the neighbors." She held the door wide open and let the men pass.

What could she have meant? Grant had thought his friend had passed away from natural causes. After all, the months in Andersonville had harmed his constitution. Starvation, disease, and dysentery were no friends to the humors. Even the sturdiest of frames couldn't withstand all of those things indefinitely. So how could this woman cry foul over Halley's death? Grant suddenly forgot why he'd wanted to see the woman as he walked down the corridor, the same way he had two days earlier when his family had just come to town.

The dining room was empty now, and the hollowness of the room was palpable. Even though he'd never seen Halley in the home, he felt his absence. The man had always been the life of a party, and Grant could well imagine that his wife missed his laughter.

She stopped in the parlor and took a place on the high-backed love seat. The piece was ornate with a dark wood trim that ran around the edge of the upholstered back like a figure eight. She didn't speak as Grant and Jesse settled themselves into chairs on the opposite side of a long squat table.

Jesse spoke first. "Mrs. Halley, did I hear you correctly? You said that your husband was kilt?" He leaned back in the chair like this was a business meeting more than an accusation of high crimes.

The woman nodded and began to weep quietly. Grant stood and offered her his kerchief. Fortunately, he had a clean one, as Julia insisted on having them washed every night.

"Did you pass this information on to anyone?" Grant didn't realize that the words had come from his mouth. He was still shocked by the woman's statement. Who would be cruel enough to murder a veteran, a man who had survived four years of hardship and torture?

Mrs. Halley shook her head. "No, who do I tell in a town this size? The sheriff's been in Higginsport. We don't have our own lawman. The mayor handles trials, but that's about all we ever have."

Bethel held only a couple hundred people at best and couldn't afford the luxuries of the county seats. County officials made do by taking other jobs. Who would pay for the extravagance of concentrated workers?

"So you just buried your man without saying a word?" Grant prodded. "Did you tell the mayor or any of your husband's friends? They would have done something." He knew that everyone in town most likely was aware that the sheriff was gone; it would be a perfect time to kill Halley. Yet, the doctor and the coroner had both ruled the death as natural.

For a second, Grant thought the widow was going to cry again or maybe leave the room. "Friends?" she finally said. "Those men are the ones that got him killed in the first place. Why would I tell them a damned thing?"

Grant leaned back in his seat. Women didn't use words like

that. He had the good graces to be embarrassed for the both of them. He cleared his throat carefully before continuing. He didn't want to provoke another unseemly outburst. "And the money?"

"Satan's filthy lucre if you ask me. I never wanted no truck with it." Mrs. Halley crossed her arms over her bosom, then slumped down on the love seat like an errant child.

"So little Jess did get the money from your house?" Grant leaned forward in his seat, resting his elbow on his leg as he listened. The conversation had taken an odd course to his intended subject.

She nodded. "I didn't want to lie, but I had no choice. Those boys weren't supposed to be in there."

"So you admit to the money?" Jesse's eyes lit up behind his gold-rimmed glasses.

Grant recognized his father's look of avarice. How many times had the man cooked up a scheme to make money while donning that same expression? If money was the root of all evil, Jesse Grant sat at its vortex.

Mrs. Halley shook her head. "I don't know much. I just know that every month, like clockwork, we got gold coins. Christopher would never tell me where they come from. I had my suspicions, but he wouldn't speak a word. He said I was better off not knowing."

Although Grant shared all the details of the household budget with Julia, he knew many homes where the wife knew nothing of the family finances. He didn't see how a military man could have effected that plan with the long periods away from home and the expenses, but Mrs. Halley seemed comfortable with the arrangement.

"When did this start?" Jesse asked. Grant watched his father's mental calculations of the money.

"When he got back in May, he had a bundle of coins. He

spent most of them, buying this place and furnishing it." She waved an ebony-gloved hand around the room to make her point.

The parlor had been filled with well-made furniture and detailed wood tables. Grant knew that this house full of city possessions had not come cheap, but unlike his father, he couldn't mentally tabulate her belongings.

"I thought that was the end of the booty," she continued, "but then in June, he had more. Not like the first time, but enough to make sure we wouldn't want for a thing. And then every month from then on."

"Where did you get the money for the pastor? Was that from the first month's coins?" Jesse had calmed down and now was leaning back in his chair, though he was still scanning the room from time to time. Most likely mentally assessing the value of the place, Grant thought.

Mrs. Halley pressed her mouth into a thin line and then opened it to speak again. "Yes. When Christopher came home with all that money and wouldn't tell me where it come from, I knew that it was blood money. So I put my foot down. We would give our tithe to the church, just as if we'd earned it honestly. He didn't dare deny the Lord His share."

Jesse nodded respectfully. With his years of sharing a home with a religious woman, he'd managed to learn how not to anger a spouse. Grant and Julia shared a less devout conviction to the Methodist church.

"That's wise, ma'am," Jesse said. "I'm sure the Lord appreciated your spirit."

"Not enough." She sniffed in such a way that Grant suspected a crying jag was not far off. "He still took my Christopher. I would have made him give it all, if I'd knowed that was the price of that money."

She picked up a figurine that looked like what Grant knew

as Dresden; Julia always raved about it. Mrs. Halley looked at the piece for a moment and let it slide from her hand to the wood floor. It splintered into a thousand tiny shards that skittered along the floor. She started to pick up another one, but Jesse snatched it from her hand. Grant knew where his father's true concern rested.

Grant harrumphed. He didn't see any divine retribution in the death of his friend. Killing came from men for selfish reasons. "So what happened to your husband? As I said before, I thought he died of natural causes."

She shook her head and pulled a handkerchief from her sleeve. She took the time to dab her eyes before speaking. "Not that I could see. He took ill after eating some meat I'd cooked. I helped him lay down. The next day I found him dead. The doctor said the meat was bad, but I know better."

Grant thought of all the men he'd seen decimated by spoiled meat and unwashed produce. Still, if Halley had withstood the conditions of Andersonville, he should have been able to fend off a piece of bad cow. His constitution should be a match for any diet after the prison camp. The men had lived on a menu of raw meat and cornmeal mixed with the occasional cornhusk. The volume of corn gave the men diarrhea, and the pork was often tainted. "It could have been some bad meat, ma'am. I've seen it do terrible things to a man."

She steeled herself to sit straight on the love seat. "It couldn't have been. I nibbled from that same piece of meat while it was cooking. Nothing was wrong with that meat."

Grant furrowed his brow. "Did you tell the doctor as much?"

She nodded again. "Of course, and the coroner as well when he examined Christopher. But who listens to the word of a woman? She's just covering up for her slovenly ways and bad cooking."

Grant knew the truth of that statement. He loved Julia

dearly, and he followed her word as gospel, but many was the time when that word had to be passed through a husband and a general in order for others to pay heed. "Well, ma'am. I hear what you have to say. I promise to take a look into this matter."

She sniffed loudly and brushed her nose with the handkerchief. "General, thank you so much. I have to apologize for my behavior. I never meant to cause your family any concern about those coins. I just don't care to ever see them again."

He nodded in sympathy. "I can understand that, but what would you have us do now? The coins are already at the parish with Reverend Evans."

Mrs. Halley managed a feeble nod. "That's fine. I didn't want them anyway. I had put them in Christopher's coffin."

CHAPTER · 6

"NO WONDER JESS wasn't more forthcoming about where he got those coins. Those boys took them from the man's coffin, no less." Jesse had begun to make a habit of discussing the case as soon as he left the front steps. The little boy's namesake looked disappointed. Even as money hungry as Jesse was, he would draw the line at grave robbing.

"That still doesn't tell us where the coins originally came from," Grant pointed out. "They came to the Halleys by way of someone."

Jesse smiled at his son. "Well, for those answers, we'll have to consult the living. Halley and Young can't tell us a thing. Unless you believe in them talking boards, now that you've been out in the world." He slapped his son on the back and started down the road.

Grant knew immediately where his father was headed, and wasn't sure that he liked the implications. Jesse was wending his way up Plane Street to Zeke Newman's house. The stately home stuck out like a thoroughbred amongst the workhorses in Bethel. If anyone knew anything, it would be Newman. Yet the thought of an interrogation made Grant cringe. The man had shown the Grants kindness by taking them in when the Halleys couldn't. How could they go into his home now and abuse his hospitality? He would be accusing his host of thievery on a grand scale.

Few crimes shy of murder and horse-thieving could be considered worse. Even if the spoils went to the victors by axiom, it didn't include making off with an entire treasury. That money rightfully belonged to the federal government, the people who had put the nation in debt to preserve a single Union.

The Confederacy had not created its own money supply. Just as they had adopted a constitution similar to the Union's, they had appropriated the coins and dies from the federal mints on Southern soil to keep their economy going. This new "country" hadn't bothered to alter the dies. They pumped out gold pieces identical to the Union's until the mints exhausted the metals. Any claims to the coins or the metals belonged with the government, no questions needed. Grant was sure that his father knew all that—and more—about the money supply. Smart merchants kept an eye on the gold market, even if there was nothing they could do to change it.

Grant's father made no pretense of where he was going. The pair went up the front steps, and Jesse rapped on the door with two knuckles. Newman answered and tried to block the view with his torso. Grant couldn't be positive in the slowly waning light of dusk, but he could have sworn that he saw Mrs. Halley inside. He shuffled to one side, but the figure had vanished. His eyes could have been playing tricks on him, but he doubted his own vision. What would Mrs. Halley be doing here so fast on the heels of their talk?

Jesse tipped his broad-brim hat at the man and smiled. "How d'you do, sir? I was wanting to thank you for taking my boy in on such short notice. It was very kindly of you to do so."

Grant watched his father. No one could be smoother when he put his mind to it. The same man who could find a way to rankle like a burr to one man with one sentence could also find a way to charm the gold out of Jeff Davis.

Newman stood aside after a few seconds. Grant knew that he still had difficulty making it around with his sticks, but he wondered if the slowness had come from wanting to stall. He wondered if this is what money did—made you suspect everyone and anyone of malice.

"Sam's one of my old friends," Newman said. "I'm happy to have him and his kin here. The house has been a mite lonely since the missus died."

Jesse stamped his feet on the mat and walked in. He wasted no time in heading for the kitchen, where Grant had seen the visitor. Could it have been Mrs. Halley? He wondered if Jesse had seen her too. She would've had to have practically run over to the house. If she'd told Newman why the Grants were coming, Jesse would be wasting his charms on the host. "Thank you. We've been out calling. It's amazing how much things have changed since I was mayor here."

Grant rolled his eyes as he passed Newman. His father just couldn't pass up an opportunity to remind others of his political past.

Newman seemed not to mind, even though Grant was sure that he remembered that time all too well. Perhaps the filter of Andersonville put the banal life of Bethel politics in perspective. Newman crutched back to the living room, where he made himself comfortable in a velvet-covered chair.

Grant couldn't help but recall how similar this seemed to the interview he and his father had conducted with Mrs. Halley. Had she told Newman about the talk, and where they sat? Had he decided to ape her actions as well as her words? Had they managed a confabulation to compare stories? Grant hesitated to think of a conspiracy amongst his old chums. It would make locating and claiming the gold that much more difficult.

He nearly stumbled over the rug that had bunched up on the floor. He was surprised that Newman would have bothered with such a nuisance, being a widower and all. Fixings were for the ladies. Still, for a bachelor, he'd done a right job at making the place a home. Beyond the accordioned hall rug, the room held Newman's velvet chair, a comfortable-looking corner seat, and a divan without a back. A small table to the side of the room held a pair of silver candleholders and a hurricane lamp.

"Where all have you been?" Newman asked as he placed the sticks against the table beside him.

Jesse cleared his throat as he settled into the chair next to Newman. Just like him to take the more comfortable seat. Grant was left with a stiff-looking divan with no place to lean back. He could practice his military straight back through the little chat.

Jesse lowered his voice a bit. "We were paying our respects to Mrs. Halley. You know how them widder women can be." The usually eloquent man had suddenly reacquired his Southern Ohio accent. Grant had to admire his father's ability to fit in almost anywhere, even if he stood out with his finery.

Newman used his arms to twist his body towards Jesse. "She's holding up quite well, considering the circumstances."

"Well, that's one of the things the general and I was worrying about. She's talking flibbertigibbet. You won't believe what she's saying." Jesse had hooked his fish with the comments.

Newman leaned forward and said in a whisper, "What is it?"

Jesse took his gold-rimmed glasses off and polished them with the tail of his shirt. "She's telling folks that her husband was murdered. Can you believe that? Everyone in town knows that he died of bad food. She's going to be causing a ruckus for nothing. Now did you ever?"

Newman bit his lower lip. Grant could see a battle big as

Antietam brewing behind his friend's brow. Newman obviously knew something but didn't want to tell these men whom he would consider outsiders despite their roots here.

"She's gonna get folks riled up, iffen she keeps at it. Bethel don't have killings here." Jesse's statement was the volley that broke the barricade.

Newman looked up in turmoil. "She's just upset. It's been a hard time for her. I'm sure she'll come to her senses soon."

"And how will a woman with children make it? She's got that big house to keep up. And the little ones to raise."

"Pshaw, Mr. Grant. You know that people around here would help a person out. Those kids won't go for nothing, you just wait and see."

Jesse shook his head in a mock sadness. Grant didn't know if he was supposed to be sad about the death of Halley or the loss of the gold coins he suspected this group hid. "Well, that's good to know. I just didn't figure that people would be taking kindly to a woman who's accusing people of murder."

Newman squinted, his eyes sliding into slits that revealed nothing. Grant knew that he had to have suspicions of where these questions were leading; Newman knew more than he was telling about Halley's death, and he also suspected this was no friendly chat with folks come calling. "I don't remember her accusing anyone of killing Chris, just that it was suspicious."

"Suspicious how?" Grant decided to get a foot into the conversation. He was tired of the careful play between these two men. He was used to being in charge and getting answers when he wanted them.

Newman seemed to snap to attention, sitting up in the chair from his conspiratorial stance with Jesse. The man looked at Grant with a frown. "Just that it was sudden. No warning. He'd had dysentery during the war, so we knew the symptoms. Hell, it's impossible not to in a place where the only flowing water is plumb full of sewage. It wasn't like that at all. One meal he's healthy as an ox, three hours later he's dead."

"Poison." Jesse threw the word into the conversation like a bomb.

Of course, if the man was dead in hours, the most likely choice was poison. That pointed directly at Mrs. Halley. Didn't she realize that she had the best opportunity to administer drugs to her husband's food? If the story started around Bethel that he had died from someone's hand, the town would look to Halley's nearest and dearest. After all, who better to tamper with the cooking? Yet, she persisted in telling the story. She could be telling the truth, or she could be trying to deflect the gossip around her husband's death. If she called it murder, people would doubt that she had a hand in the doings. Just as Grant was questioning those facts now.

Newman nodded. "It would have to be poison. It wasn't pretty. He was shaking and thrashing around. He threw up all the food in him—and then some. Then all of a sudden, he stopped. That was worse than the jumping around, by far."

Grant hung his head. In all his years in the Army, even when he crossed the Isthmus of Panama while struggling with soldiers who had contracted malaria, he'd never heard of a disease that mimicked those symptoms. "But the doctor?"

"The old bones in town must be eighty if he's a day. He could barely find his way into the house, much less tell Mrs. Halley what Christopher died of. And the coroner, Doc Adolph, wasn't about to contradict his old friend Peck. You're used to more modern medical care than what's we got here." As Newman looked down at the stump of his leg, Grant wondered what he was thinking.

Had he received good care in the Army? Had they tried everything to save the leg, or had the doctor merely sawed it off to save himself a few hours of care? In the heat of battle, many soldiers received expedient treatment. Grant didn't even want to imagine what the Andersonville infirmary had meted out in the name of healing.

He wanted to shove the reminders of what war had wrought on so many people. For some it had brought disability and hardship; for him it had brought fame and good fortune. He had a political career and perhaps the presidency in his future. What of Newman? What did he have? No wife and no leg. Halley and Young had no lives.

"Do you think it's poison?" Grant asked.

"Could be. Not sure that I'd run around town saying as much, but it could be." Newman leaned back against the chair as if he'd been released from a burden. The tight grip that he'd held on himself seemed to leave his body in a moment. Once again, he was the genial host and the friend from years gone by.

Jesse cleared his throat, clearly expecting a libation, as it was getting to be the time of day for a round of pre-dinner drinks. Newman would be hard-pressed to mix and pour with his sticks. Grant didn't know a kindly manner of asking if he needed help. Some folks took well to it; others saw it as an insult. He didn't want to appear too anxious for the drinks. People spread rumors about his liquor habits. Demanding a drink would only fuel the stories.

He hadn't finished his thought when the colored woman came in with a pitcher of lemonade and some glasses. Grant sighed. Three men should be able to enjoy the finer things in life without interference. The woman poured without a word and settled the tray by Newman. He handed out the drinks and took a bite of one of the cookies she'd brought out.

"Patsy doesn't hold much truck with drinking and booze. But she makes a mean cookie, for sure." Newman lifted his glass in a toast. "To fallen comrades, Sam. May we keep their memories alive."

Grant took a swig of the lemonade and made a face. How in tarnation could folks like Rutherford and Lucy Hayes drink this all day long? He'd have a sour puss by the time night rolled around. "I heard that Young didn't make it either. What happened?" Though the question was plain enough, Grant wondered if the man had been murdered as well. If strange goings-on were afoot here, it would be just as possible that two men had been killed as one.

"Got his face blown off by a Reb." Newman bit down hard on the cookie, and tiny crumbs littered the rug around him. "We were two days out of Andersonville when it happened. We'd made our way down to the coast of Georgia by accident. Got turned around. Couple of the men wanted to see first-hand what Sherman had done. The rest just wanted to stretch their legs after all that time in prison. Then we started back up towards Atlanta—or what was left of it."

Grant nodded. He knew too well the path of devastation that Sherman had forced on the South as he marched through Georgia. No army had ever attempted such a bold move through enemy territory. The mass destruction was without precedent. Bombs could never wreak that much havoc. "How did he get shot then?"

"We were a bit south of Atlanta still, when a raiding party of Rebs came through. They wanted to take our rations and horses. When we put up a fuss about it, one of them drew a gun and shot Young about point-blank." Newman shivered as if a cat had walked over his grave.

The horrors of war would most likely haunt the men of their generation. Perhaps the thought of destruction could bring peace for the next few decades. Grant couldn't imagine more violence in the country or against a president. Even so, there was talk of more war in Mexico, dealing with the French and their puppet government. Violence seemed to never sleep.

"That's about all to tell," Newman continued. "The other men got scared when they saw what that Reb had done. They took off, and the shooter did the same. We buried Young in a local cemetery and came on home."

Jesse shook his head and mimicked the *tsking* noises like Hannah made so often. "What a shame. Just to get out of that misery and not be able to enjoy it. You didn't have enough supplies to make his death worth fighting for."

"So it was definitely an act of war?" Grant asked. The thought that the deaths were all related had started to form in his head. If Mrs. Halley suspected murder, then perhaps Young's death was foul play. All the main suspects had been at the scene of the first death, but from Newman's account, they all seemed to give each other an alibi.

"That's true. We were definitely down on our luck." Newman picked up his glass and started to take a sip. The whiz of a bullet crashed through the front pane and smashed through his drink before he could bring it to his lips. One moment, he held a glass of lemonade; the next, he fumbled with shards as they slipped from his fingers. The yellow liquid dripped from his hand, but he didn't seem to be hit.

Grant dropped to the floor from instinct. Newman made an awkward flop on the rug in front of him.

Jesse didn't bother to duck for cover. The oldest of the group stood up as if he'd been personally insulted and stormed to the window like Pickett on a charge.

Chapter 7

JESSE FLICKED THE CURTAIN aside and looked out the window.

Grant tried to lunge at his father, but he was too far away to pull the man down. "What are you doing? You could be killed."

Jesse looked down on him—as he had so many times when Grant was a child—and his face drooped in disappointment. Grant momentarily reflected on the time he'd gone to bid on a horse. When the farmer had asked him what he would pay, Grant repeated Jesse's exact instructions on bidding on the beast, including his opening and final bids. The story had made the rounds of Georgetown's villagers for weeks. Jesse had looked down on him then and instructed him never to repeat business instructions to anyone.

Now he stood by the window with the exact same look on his face. "It's not like he's going to stand out there, Ulysses. Someone might take a single shot through the window, but no one is fool enough to stand out there, waiting to be noticed. Lest you forget, you can get arrested for shooting guns off in the town limits."

Grant crawled on all fours to the window. "What's out there?" Despite his father's insistence, it wouldn't be the first time Jesse had been wrong about something.

Jesse tugged at his son under his arm. "Nothing and no one. The street is empty."

Grant stood up and brushed off his knees, though there was very little dust on them. Newman's help must do a spotless job of cleaning. "Humph, that's just the way. No one is around when you need them."

They both turned to look at Newman, who was struggling to pull himself up using the chair for leverage. Grant hurried over to the man and offered an arm for support.

Newman reached up and used it to help get himself back on his sticks. He wobbled a bit as he tried to lead his guests to the kitchen.

The room was empty, and Grant wondered for a moment if the help had skedaddled at the sound of the gunshot. Rural Ohio had been spared the worst of the war, despite being so close to Kentucky and the South. Except for the random hunter, men didn't fire weapons in town—even places as small as Bethel. That could change, though, with all the guns being brought home from the war.

Newman didn't stop at the table or the sink. Instead, he headed for the door and shoved it back using his stick. He managed the steps and started off into the grass without waiting for his guests.

Jesse looked to follow him, but Grant wasn't sure what was going on. Was Newman going to hide from future surprise attacks, or was he going to confront the shooter?

Newman looked back at them. "I think it's about time we talked with someone. I don't like where this is going."

Grant decided that it might be in his best interest to follow his friend. He wasn't sure how this tied into little Jess and the gold coins, but he wanted to clear his son of any wrongheaded accusations. The coins seemed to be at the bottom of all the strange doings in Bethel.

Jesse caught up with Newman and looked at the man. "Where are we going? Who can tell you who would be taking potshots at you?"

"I don't know that he will. But he was with us when we came home from Andersonville, and maybe he can shed some light on this."

Grant caught up with them and gasped in a few deep breaths. He wasn't used to having to deal with civilians in the face of gunfire. He preferred to be in charge when men were shooting at him. He fought back the temptation to bark out some orders. "Who are we going to see? Micah Brown or Adam Woerner?"

Newman's gaze lingered on him with hooded eyes. He must not have been expecting anyone to figure out the connection between the men, but to a military man, the code and the camaraderie were understood. Men from the same company stuck together. If one of them had gold, the rest of the group knew about it and likely had some too.

"Woerner," he answered. "He's mentioned something about some poachers. I need to talk to him."

Grant doubted the story. He bet Newman wanted to share his suspicions with one of his partners. He'd have to, with all this killing going on. A gunshot through the front window, coming on top of rumors that Halley had been murdered—it made a man question who his friends were. The gunshot would make Newman check up on his so-called friends and see where their true loyalites lay.

Grant didn't respond to the comments, but kept pace with the man. He wanted to hear what transpired from the upcoming conversation.

For whatever reasons, Jesse didn't speak either. Perhaps the shooting had shaken him, or he didn't know how to react to such bald-faced lies. The crunch of Newman's sticks against the pebbles on the road intruded on their silence.

When they reached what Grant assumed to be the Woerner place, Jesse let out a soft whistle. If the two other houses had been grand, this one was beyond superlatives. The home looked as though it had been picked up from New York City and dropped in the middle of this hamlet. Grant flashed back to his first visit to the Executive Mansion. Even then, he just strolled up to the White House and went in like any other well-wisher for the Lincolns. That experience was the only comparison he could make to the home he saw now.

The front of the house stretched out through the lawn in both directions, with a wide portico marking the center. The brick walls had snippets of vine starting up the sides, which only accentuated its airs of newness. A paved walk stretched from the brilliant white door to the steps down to the yard and out to the dirt street. Glazed windows peered emotionless on the town.

Grant wondered what Bethel's citizens thought of such opulence. How could they not know that these men had returned flush with money? Townsfolk knew everyone's business. They would see the wealth and want to know more about these parvenus. No one could blame the town for its curiosity. These men hadn't made any bones about hiding it.

Newman crutched up the walk to the front door. The paving made his trek easier, and Grant wondered why he didn't install the same convenience for himself. Money should at least be used to make life easier.

Newman was already pounding on the front door by the time the Grants reached the steps to the front porch. The trio stood in the shade of the columns, waiting for a response. Grant tried to listen for indications of a man inside the house, but he was greeted only with silence.

Despite having heard battle more times than he could count, Grant found that the still of a moment could be infinitely more frightening. The uncertainty and the unease of not knowing what was to come next could chill his blood like no mortar or bullet's whiz could. Those sounds he knew and recognized.

Newman grabbed the door handle and threw it open. Grant wasn't surprised that the door wasn't locked. Even if the entire Mint of the United States sat in the foyer, locking the door would have been unthinkable. People didn't even consider trying to lock out crime. There had been no theft, until now when men had brought home horrors and nightmares—and guns.

The Grants followed Newman single-file into the house, watching for any signs of interest from the neighbors. Grant came up short to avoid running smack into Newman. Jesse bumped into his son and sidestepped to see why the procession had stopped. Grant went to the other side of Newman's sticks, and his mouth dropped open.

The body at the base of the staircase was undoubtedly dead. His neck had been broken; no one could be that flexible in life. Even though the body's chest lay flat on the tile floor, the head snapped to look at the chandelier.

Grant recognized Woerner without asking for identification from Newman. He remembered the diminutive man from their days in Bethel. One of the few men in this part of the country actually shorter than Grant, the little fellow had been known for carrying a cheroot in his mouth at all times. Grant scanned the floor but saw no signs of a cigar anywhere. As a young man, Woerner had taken the cigar out only long enough to toss down hard whiskey or steal a kiss from some pretty young miss. Grant wondered if the prison camp had cured him of the cigar habit.

The room was silent as a tomb as Grant started to look around. He started with the body and circled the corpse in ever-widening rings. Nothing looked out of place or out of sorts. Maybe Woerner had the same woman that Newman used. The tile was shiny clean. The stairs were wide and free of any kind of toys that would be found at the Grant home after a day with little Jess.

At first glance, Grant could see no reason for Woerner's fatal fall. He made his way back to the body and leaned down by the man.

Jesse had taken a seat in one of the austere wooden chairs by the door. Grant recognized it as the type of chair Julia would tell him was only for show, never sitting. Judging from Jesse's pallor, he wasn't concerned with protocol at the moment. For as much livestock as he'd slaughtered, the elder Grant had little experience with violent human death. He seemed to have a bad case of the collywobbles.

Newman rested against the opposite jamb of the door, propping his weight against the painted wood.

Grant bent over the body and inhaled. The stench of death had already started to overtake Woerner, wrapping him in a cloak of urine and decay. The general knew the smell only too well after four years of war. Still, he didn't catch any vapors of the demon liquor, as his mother would call it. Woerner hadn't been drunk when he took the tumble down the stairs. The man's body was whole, unmarked by the ravages of war as Newman's had been. If he wasn't drunk and not maimed, Grant couldn't figure out why a healthy man of 40 would plummet headfirst down the stairs.

He knew one reason, and he decided to try to push it out of his noggin. No use in speculating on what had happened. Guessing just got a man in trouble. Still, three men of Bethel were dead now. Three men who had gone off to fight, been captured, and sent to Andersonville. Three men who had shared a secret about gold. The situation was trouble like an open fire in a stable.

Once the doubt came in, there was no getting rid of it. The questions were like an uninvited houseguest who came in and put his shoes up on the best furniture. You couldn't ask him nicely to leave.

Grant had a suspicion that it was more than coincidence that three men were murdered and someone had tried to shoot at Newman. He knew of whole Federal brigades with fewer casualties than this village of two hundred souls. A few more deaths would make this a widow town.

He took a look around the room again, without spotting anything different. Woerner's home was expansive but plain. No possession made it unique or naturally his. Grant missed the photos and paintings that marked his own home.

Jesse apparently couldn't stand the inactivity and stood up to pace. He lurched back and forth through the foyer, stopping each time at the front door to look out on Plane Street.

"Is anyone out there?" Grant wanted to know what was so fascinating outside, when a murder had just occurred inside the home. If his father took the time to look inside the house, he'd get more excitement than he bargained for.

Jesse turned to look at his son and shook his head. His eyes had retreated into their sockets, and he looked older than he had ten minutes before. The killing had dimmed the driving spirit that seemed to hurtle him through any situation. Grant wondered if he was just now starting to realize that a murderer lurked among the people they had called neighbors and friends.

"Nobody there, and not likely to be," Jesse said. "I'll have to let the mayor know to inform Doc Adolph about the death, but I can't make any promises about what will happen when Crosson gets back from Higginsport. He may have a few ideas of his own on looking into all these deaths."

Grant knew that to be true. The tiny township governments

in Clermont County had longstanding rivalries. It was always easier to pick on the weaknesses of someone else. Grant bet that Sheriff Crosson from Wayne Township would be more inclined to take on Bethel's new money than to tangle with Wayne Township's prominent families. The stakes were a lot lower in the next village over. That would give them only a few days to figure out what was going on before the sheriff came in, guns waving and making accusations.

Woerner had been dead for at least a few hours, time enough for a man to come, go, and get a good piece towards Cincinnati or Columbus. It was a vain hope to expect the killer to remain in the house. Even with those thoughts, Grant knew that the killer lived here. A place like Bethel noticed a man who left town suddenly almost as much as it spotted a stranger in its midst.

Grant started to mount the stairs, taking each step with trepidation as if the same lethal fate might befall him. He watched his feet as he rose above the marble floor, but the steps were wide and easy to navigate. No reason for a man to trip.

He had almost made it to the upper landing, when he noticed chipped paint on the stair railing. He hunkered down to take a look-see at the mark. It stood out in the newness of everything around it. On closer investigation, Grant noticed a thin line which ran around the pole about four inches off the carpet. He looked for some sign of what might have caused the indentation.

He turned around to look at the pole on the opposite side of the staircase, almost knowing what would be there. It took him a few seconds, as the two poles didn't match up exactly in relationship to the top of the stairs. But it was there. Another thin line ran around the bottom of the post.

Grant found no sign of what had caused the indentations. He knew, though. The wood looked as if a wire had been tied around it and pulled taut. Just like it would if Woerner had tripped across a wire and fallen. This was entirely too coincidental, especially on top of all the events that preceded Woerner's death.

The grooves could have been made at any time by anyone. They didn't have to be made at this house. Even if he could show that it had caused Woerner's death, Grant couldn't prove the time that the trap had been set. Anyone could have planned to kill the man just as had been done with Halley. This killer hadn't seemed to be in a big hurry to finish off the group in the beginning. Almost six months had passed between Young's death and the death of Halley. Grant wondered why two attempts had now been made so fast on the heels of Halley. Why the urgency at this time?

Grant knew of only one person who might answer that. Newman had been with the others at Andersonville. Their time in confinement had something to do with what was going on in Bethel. Grant knew it.

CHAPTER · 8

GRANT MOVED INTO THE LIBRARY of Woerner's house and motioned Newman in after him. The man took his time in coming, like a pupil who knew the schoolmarm had it in for him. In this case, the punishment seemed to be sudden unexplained death, not sentences on the chalkboard. Newman's fantod only made Grant more resolute to get it over with.

Newman shut the door behind him. Jesse seemed to have vanished, but Grant wasn't sure if he'd left or if he'd found some bauble to catch his interest. It would be entirely in keeping with his father for the man to boast of how he'd found Woerner's body and then charge two bits to see the remains. Grant didn't put much past his father's keen sense of making a pretty penny. After all, Jesse had made a killing during the war with wholesale leather and cotton.

"So what do you make of the body out there?" Grant faced the glazed windows, looking out at the manicured lawn and the dirt street beyond it. Bethel must have been shocked at the expense that went into these homes. They put his father's house—once Tom Morris's place—to shame. The townsfolk were given to plain talk and simple homes. People in these parts like to keep social position on an equal footing. But now five men had thrown the balance out of kilter.

Newman shrugged his well-developed shoulders. "Not much to think. The man's dead. Seen enough of those to know what it looks like."

Grant rounded the back of the chair and moved so that he was directly in front of his friend. He grabbed the chair's arms to block the man from leaving and stared deep into Newman's eyes. He could see a glimmer of fear under the bushy brows. "What about the money?"

For a second, Newman stammered and scanned the room for assistance. Grant followed his eyes, but there was no one save the two of them. And the dead man in the next room, who served as a reminder of what was happening here. Finally, Newman set his sticks aside and rested in the stiff-backed chair.

"It's no coincidence," Grant said, "that the men who came home from the war with money in their pockets are the same ones who are dying, is it?"

Newman sunk back in the cushion of the chair as if the general would strike him.

No use in letting him think otherwise, Grant thought. Any resource that would break this code of silence should be used.

"No, it's not." Newman swallowed hard.

Grant stood up straight again. Just as in war, once the line had been breached, it was only a matter of time until the troops would be triumphant. Newman's defenses were broken now, and the general could take his time in getting the full story. He'd seen it happen many times with prisoners of war. Rebs captured by the troops would talk just to have someone listen. Still, even in the darkest, bloodiest days of the war, he would never have treated his prisoners the way that the men in Andersonville suffered. Behind all his Southern manners, Bobby Lee could be a brute.

Grant looked around for a drink and spied a set of crystal

decanters on the sofa table. *Figures that even the hooch is gussied up in this place,* he thought. "Why don't you start at the beginning of the story," he prodded. "It happened after you got out of Andersonville?"

Grant lifted a decanter from the mirrored tray. He poured two tumblers of what he assumed was mash whiskey. Without the labels, he had to go by what his nose told him. They were close enough to whiskey country for Woerner to procure the good stuff.

Newman nodded and extended his hand for the glass. Grant willingly offered it, wanting to hear his friend's story. If only the fortifications of Vicksburg had been breached so easily.

"Go on." Grant sat down in the seat opposite Newman and watched the man take a belt of the whiskey.

The liquor seemed to settle something inside of him, and he wiped his mouth with the back of his sleeve. "Well, it was just after we left that place. You'll never know what it was like there. The death. The waste. I'll never forget it. It's hell to see your friends starve to death and not be able to lift a hand to help." Newman sniffed out loud, and Grant wondered if the big man would start bawling. Nothing he hated worse than seeing a grown man weep.

"So where did the money come from?" Grant wanted this interview over with. The sooner he knew the truth about the money, the sooner he could put an end to these needless deaths. He was due in Cincinnati in a few days for more parades and parties. It wouldn't do to be late for functions in his honor. Moreover, Crosson would be back, and who knew what the sheriff would do with the murders and the gold? Newman was a very apt and noticeable suspect. Grant didn't want the small-town lawman to settle on the most convenient suspect.

"Well, we started back to Ohio. The five of us. Young was in the best shape of us all. They didn't send him there until last winter. By then, I'd been in almost nine months. He rode ahead of us, making sure that we didn't run into any trouble."

Grant nodded. So many families in the North thought that just because Lee had surrendered, the war was over. Fighting had gone on for weeks after Appomattox. A few generals thought that a last-minute victory might change their fortunes heading into peacetime or gain them notoriety that could be used for political gain. People liked a winner. Hadn't Andy Jackson made it to the presidency based on a battle fought after the treaty was signed?

"Well, apparently, we'd got turned around," Newman continued. "On the second day, we figured out that we were south of Atlanta and needed to head back north. Young had got a ways ahead of us, scouting out for some grub, when we heard a gunshot, then a second. By the time we got to where Young was, it was too late. Some Reb had shot him, blown half his face clean off."

Grant bowed his head. The shame was that the dying had continued after the end of the war. After so many had gone on to their rewards, you'd think that the rest would be able to celebrate a few years of life before meeting their Maker. But as soon as the war was over, things returned to normal. That meant death and birth and all the other experiences that had been forgotten while the nation struggled. "So what about the second shot? Young took two bullets?"

Newman looked down at the floor, studying the varnished planks. "Nope, he'd managed to kill the Reb who shot him. We found the Reb, laying on the ground and spitting up blood. He trained his gun on Halley and was going to shoot him."

"But Halley didn't get shot."

"Nope, Woerner shot the gun clean out of his hand and then demanded to know why the Reb had shot Young."

"A lot of men didn't know the war was over. It happened

with more frequency than I'd care to admit." Grant swirled the tumbler and tried to resist the temptation of the liquor. He had to get to the bottom of this mystery before he got to the bottom of the glass. Once he started downing the whiskey, he'd want to polish off the bottle cleaner than Patsy could with her elbow grease.

"The Reb was slumped against a wagon. We made a move to check it out, and the Reb tried to stop us. Apparently a couple of his pals had left him there to guard the goods while they scavenged for food. Young had happened on him and lost the fight. We could tell that the Reb wasn't going to last much longer, so we asked him what was worth shooting men over. And he said, 'gold.'"

Grant closed his eyes for a minute. He knew what the fever did to men. Gold was the great equalizer of the previous two decades. Ever since that metal had been found at Sutter's Mill, people had wanted to find a cache of it and be the next society family. One panful of muddy water might change a man's life. So they dipped into the ground until they found it or they became a part of that same land.

If gold was involved in this case, no telling how far people would go to get it and keep it. Grant had been stationed on the West Coast to keep the peace at the height of the gold fever there. He'd seen firsthand what greed could do to grown men, make them fight and squabble for a few nuggets. No telling what men would do for the Confederate treasury.

"Turns out that the Reb had been in Richmond with Jeff Davis and the last of his government. They'd headed to Danville when Richmond fell and to parts south after Lee surrendered. The troops were in such a dither that a few wagonloads of the gold got separated—or so the Reb said. I wouldn't be too surprised if the gold had a bit of help in getting separated from the rest."

Grant nodded. Times in the South would not be pleasant for a while to come. Though some people favored a quick reunion with the wayward states, many of the Radical Republicans wanted a more formal and exacting reentry into the Union. The common folk trying to eke out a living off the red soil were likely to find conditions worse before they got better. The currency was worthless. Inflation ran amok, and gold prices were a fraction of what they'd been before the war. Hard currency would go a long ways to easing the money worries. Davis had parceled out some of the gold coins to his troops before he sent them home to face the terrible conditions left by Union occupation.

"Anyways, the Reb told us that Jeff Davis and the rest of his cohorts had headed south to Florida, but they couldn't follow since they had no maps or compasses. So they decided to head home."

Grant knew how Reb deserters had left in droves at the end of the war. Desperation and a growing sense of the inevitability of defeat hadn't helped morale or the spirit of the troops. They'd suspected defeat since Gettysburg and known it since Atlanta. They knew the futility of fighting, even if Davis hadn't. The Federals had saved months of fighting the South because men were leaving the front lines at a high rate. "So the troops were on their way home when you came upon them?"

Newman looked away, staring through the windows to the bucolic little town. Grant wondered what he saw there—the ghosts of his friends and his dead wife? Or was he remembering the moment when he had decided to join ranks with the others to take that gold? One of those moments that changed a life for good. So many people had passed on, and yet life was expected to continue as if nothing had happened. Hannah had schooled him well at hiding emotions, but even he longed for some of the friends he'd lost in battle.

Newman cleared his throat and looked down at his now-empty tumbler. Grant took the hint and rose to refill it. Their host wouldn't be objecting if they helped themselves to a bit more hooch. He splashed some more of the amber liquid into the glass and made a pretense of topping off his own. Newman didn't seem to care if Grant drank or not, so long as he listened.

Handing the glass back to Newman, Grant took a tiny swallow from his own glass and sat down quietly, waiting for the story to recommence. Having a taste made him want all of it. He heard the chirping of a bird, one of God's creatures that knew nothing of war or murder. The birds just lived the cycle of life without care for what the humans did to each other.

Newman downed about half the glass. Grant tried to look calm and patient, as though he could understand the point of the story. A look of contempt or judgment at this juncture might send the man running back into his shell. He wanted the whole story so he could cotton what was going on.

"Well, the Reb said that his buddies would be back, but to be honest, he didn't act like a man waiting on reinforcements. Later, Halley said that he thought the man might have kilt the other Rebs to get the gold all to himself. You can't trust them graybacks for nothing."

"So what happened to the Reb? Did you let him go?" Grant didn't know what Halley or Newman was capable of in that situation. No telling what that Reb soldier had done to secure the gold from Jeff Davis's wagon train. No situation like that had presented itself to them as young men in Bethel. Perhaps the Reb had followed them home and started taking his revenge on the group for stealing the gold.

"He died about then. So it was the four of us and a wagon-load of gold. We loaded up the horses with as much as we could carry, then buried the rest. Figured we was set for life that way.

No one would be able to figure out what had happened to it. Those Reb boys couldn't have found their—well, you know what—with both hands."

Grant raised an eyebrow; apparently Newman remembered the general's distaste for cursing. He looked around the room at the paneled walls and the dark furniture. Leather-bound books that had never been opened, much less read. Money had bought all this for Woerner, but had taken his life. Had it been a good trade in Woerner's eyes?

"So we came back here. We each took a bit of money to start with and hid the rest for later. We figured we'd dole out some here and there to get us by. It got to be a monthly thing. We'd take a few coins out and use them to live on for the month. We didn't have to worry about crops or rain or locusts or flies. We lived a life of leisure."

Grant winced at the thought. Part of the missing Confederate treasury was right here in Bethel with his friends. He could see the newspapers making a fuss over the scandal now. Lincoln had wanted to use the money to pay down part of the obligations incurred from the war. The national debt ran into the millions of dollars, a sum that Grant couldn't even get his mind around. Besides, the Confederate gold had been coined from the U.S. mints on Southern soil. The Feds had owned all of it before the war. The moves had given rise to a cadre of speculators and financiers who'd grown fat off the suffering of a nation.

The war had wrought monumental changes in the way cash was handled in the country. Lincoln had brought all the states under a single currency, removing all the different paper money that the various states had issued for years. He'd removed the gold backing from the greenbacks, creating inflation like never before.

Newman finished off his whiskey. "We figured that Jeff Davis didn't need all that gold where he was going. After all, he'd hid it somewheres with his books. He was more interested in getting away."

Davis had kept meticulous records of the final days of his regime and had carted those off with the gold, in hopes of continuing the war from the Western frontier. His war journals had been lost along with the gold, or so everyone thought. He'd wanted war at all costs, including guerrilla tactics. Many in the North suspected that he'd not been quite right in the head in those final months of the war. The journals could prove the point one way or the other. Many members of the Confederate Cabinet breathed a sigh of relief that they'd not been found. Who would want to be serving a crazy man? Those journals and records would show people that he'd not seen the reality of the Confederacy's demise.

Grant nodded. Jeff Davis had left a good part of his men and jumped into a skirt to hide out from the Feds, or so the stories went. While Grant had worn a skirt at West Point to play Desdemona, he'd done that only at the insistence of men like Sherman and Julia's brother Fred. It was a mockery of valor to try to escape behind a shawl.

"So you split the money up four ways?" Grant tried to think of how much money they could carry back to Bethel from Georgia. Gold wasn't a load of feathers. The horses would need lots of food and water for such a heavy trip.

Newman shook his head. "Nothing that simple. Woerner came up with a plan. We'd store the money all in one place and dole it out in bits and pieces every month."

"So you never had your part of the money?" Grant wondered how the men could trust each other so implicitly. Maybe he'd dealt with Washington too long. He didn't know how he could allow someone else to save his gold.

"Not really. Woerner took care of it. After all, his daddy ran the store for years, so he knowed all about making change and counting money. We just let him do it."

"So did the widow Halley get her share after Christopher was killed?" Grant started to see motives for murder spring up all around him. Still, each motive applied to only one person or one family. He couldn't see the reasons for killing the different men when no one person profited.

Newman shook his head again. He was beginning to remind Grant of little Jess when someone caught him in the cookie jar. "Nope, nothing like that either. Woerner set things up in a tontine. When one person died, the money went to the survivors, and it would be doled out from there. No one would own the money until only one person was left."

Grant would have cursed under his breath if he weren't a God-fearing man. The last thing he wanted to think of was his friends slaughtering each other. They had survived bad weather, poor health, and no vittles to come back home—not to kill each other over money. With this bit of information, it all came back to the men who'd returned from Andersonville. Each one of them had a perfect motive for murdering the rest. As if money wasn't bad enough for ruining friendships, they had made it lethal with a survivorship clause.

"So we got the money each month. A few people asked questions, but only because we bought the biggest houses in town and started driving the nice carriages. Mrs. Halley almost upset the apple cart when she tithed, but we convinced the parson not to ask too many questions. Other than that, life went on." Newman's eyes didn't flutter at the last phrase.

Grant couldn't tell if he had meant that as a joke or not. Life certainly didn't go on for three of the men who had found the bounty. "So what happens to Young's widow? And Mrs. Halley? Are they left without a cent now?" He thought it cruel that these women had come so close to luxury, only to be done out of it by men's greed. But so often women went without.

Grant had seen women evicted from homes and left to walk the streets in the aftermath of a husband's death.

"They'll get a little something. The married men did want something for the families. It's only right."

Grant nodded. *As it should be*, he thought. He'd make sure that Julia was always prepared for, no matter what. He always had his military pension to rely on. At least, Julia would never go without again. "Well, you're not going to appreciate this, but I need to take possession of this money. I'm afraid it's taken too many lives already, and it belongs to the federal government." If found with the gold, those Confederate diaries could be used to try Jeff Davis for treason.

Newman grabbed his sticks and looked like he might try to bolt. Fat lot of good that would do the man. He adjusted himself in the chair and turned to face Grant. "I can't do that."

"I know what you're going to say about your friends and the trust they place in you."

Newman looked him square in the eyes, and Grant wondered for a moment if the man might cry. "It's not that, Sam. I would if I could. But Woerner took the money and hid it. The only man who knows where the treasure lays is at the bottom of the steps, dead."

CHAPTER · 9

GRANT WOULD HAVE HAD an easier time trying to rout Sherman's march single-handedly than convincing his family not to participate in a treasure hunt. He saw a sparkle in his father's eyes that boded an ill wind coming his way. Jesse would be the first in line to improve his lot in life. Grant winced to think of what the man would do with that much gold. He'd be incorrigible, flaunting the wealth, and yet he'd still want more. Every step up in his business had resulted in a move to a new town and a bigger audience for his growing notoriety. He'd have a house in Covington that would make these look like shanties.

And little Jess was no better. He had pulled some nonsense penny dreadful from the bookshelves at Newman's house and started reciting passages about hidden staircases and dastardly villains who tried to stop the hero from finding the cache of gold. Patsy had listened patiently as the boy read aloud, but Julia had none of it. She'd confiscated the book, but not before the damage had set in. The lad had woken the household at seven in the morning, dragging a spade up the stairs, clanking like a dinner bell.

Given the sparse clues to the gold's whereabouts, Newman and Grant decided to start with Woerner's house. The coins had to be somewhere easily accessible, since they were doled out every month, but hidden so as not to be found by someone with an eye for such things. Villages were stocked with nosy neighbors and prying spinsters.

Woerner's home seemed an ideal place for the gold. He'd lived alone, so he had no meddlesome family to find the treasure. Grant envied the dead man's wealth as the pack entered the opulent house for the second day in a row.

The body had been removed. Woerner's only relation was a maiden aunt in Felicity, and the mayor had seen to taking care of the preparations. Dr. Adolph Shroen lived over in Ohio Township of Clermont County, and the body had been transported there. Grant knew that any hints to the cause of death would be lost on the bumpy ride over. He had seen no reason for keeping the corpse around; Woerner wasn't planning on telling them much. Someone had tripped him with a wire and left him to fate.

Although Newman and the Grants were prepared for reconnoitering, no one seemed to have a plan for locating the gold, short of ripping the house to shreds. Grant parceled out scouting missions, falling into his role as general and strategizer. He gave Jess the basement in order to let the lad use his cacophonic shovel, and sent Jesse to supervise. Assigning Newman to the first floor, he would take the second with Julia. He thought his wife, with her feminine wiles, would be of most help in the upstairs living quarters.

As the pair mounted the stairs, Grant paused to show Julia the booby trap he'd discovered. She gave it a moment's thought and could fathom no domestic reason for the grooves. Grant was disappointed; he'd half hoped that she would make a reasonable household excuse, so they could forget the thoughts of murder.

The Grants started with the master bedroom. He rued that

he and Julia had not been able to spend more time together. She was more than a wife or helpmate to him. She was his rock and worth more than all Croesus's gold.

Julia quickly fluffed the pillows and mattress but found no sign of the gold. The search went fast. The places that a person could hide a wagonload of gold were few and far removed in a house of any size. Grant looked under the beds and in the closets for anything that could hold large quantities of gold. Woerner would want to keep it all in a single place. One good hiding location would be easier to come by than multiple locales in Bethel. Grant counted that fact among the fortunes of having the money hidden in a small town.

He methodically went from room to room, searching cubbyholes, under the beds, closets, and any space where a sack of gold might fit.

Newman had trusted Woerner and had no idea how much gold had originally existed or how much remained after the distribution. Jesse had guessed it at $35,000. Grant knew that his father wouldn't be far wrong. That was a fair number of double eagles.

Although Grant doubted it, the men could have run out of gold, making the search fruitless. The timing would be too coincidental for his taste. From the stories he'd heard in Washington, there was still enough gold left to fill a few rooms in a home.

He'd almost finished one of the three guest rooms, when Julia came out of the master bedroom with a family Bible cradled in her hands. Grant hoped that she hadn't decided that prayer was the only solution to their current dilemma. He favored a more active approach.

"Ulys, come look at this." She held open the book to a particular page that had been marked in the Bible.

Grant took the book and peered at it. The marker had set the page to St. Luke, Chapter 19. Though he was more familiar with St. Matthew's version of the parable of the talents, he knew the passage from his days as a boy with his mother, who had drummed the Scripture into her family at every opportunity.

Grant started to read and stopped immediately. As the servants brought back what they were given plus some, he could easily see the similarities in the story to their current predicament. Yet it was hubris for Woerner to compare himself to the master. In the parable, the master was equated to God, the Supreme Being. Had Woerner possessed some hold over the others that allowed him to keep the money and pass it out like a father does an allowance to his children?

"I think it's a hint," Julia said triumphantly.

Grant had to grudgingly agree. He considered any mention of gold suspicious. The tale was close enough to his friends' situation that it couldn't be coincidence. Had Woerner just found amusement in the likeness, or had he left a suggestion to where the gold was buried?

The passage talked about the servants who traded and put the money in the bank as well as the bad servant who had hidden his coin in a napkin. Grant tried to imagine a napkin big enough to carry the gold trove, but it would need to be the size of a tablecloth.

Would Woerner call himself a bad servant? What of servants? Halley's housekeeper had to suspect now, with all the dying going on. And what would Patsy gain from these deaths? The questions made his head ache.

"So what now?" Julia asked, as if her husband would know the next steps to take based on a Bible verse.

The parable was little help. Wasn't St. Luke the book that talked about the blind leading the blind as well? Grant felt quite sightless in this matter. Perhaps another trip to Reverend Evans would be in order. A man of the cloth would be more familiar with the passage and might shed some light on what it could mean in terms of finding the gold.

Julia led the way downstairs, hefting the massive tome like it was a tablet. Grant brought up the rear, fully expecting to see everyone else long since finished with their toils. He took care with each step, watching for other wires or traps. No one waited for them on their arrival at the foot of the stairway. Grant shivered a moment, thinking of how his friend had broken his neck on these same stairs just a day prior.

He scanned the room again, wondering what had made someone kill Woerner. Was it the thought of a larger share of gold? Would the whole of the Confederate treasury be enough for someone who thought that way? The killer already possessed more than he could spend in a lifetime in a town like Bethel.

Grant was shaken from his thoughts by the return of Newman. The man had a look on his face that Grant couldn't read; his eyes drooped, but he moved along at such a pace with his sticks that Grant couldn't believe that melancholia had struck him.

Between his index finger and thumb of his left hand, the man carried a small golden key. He held on to it tight as he made his way to the foyer. He came to a stop and rested on a small bench in the entryway. "Maybe we should wait for your father before we talk about all this."

The patter of feet against stairs interrupted the men, and Grant knew it would only be seconds before they could talk. Jesse looked out of breath as he entered from the back of the house.

Little Jess came running into the room, smeared with dirt and grime. Traces of cobwebs laced his hair like a bonnet. He'd obviously been sweating as he dug in the cellar. "Papa, look." He held out a filthy hand to show a coin.

Grant took it and held it towards the front windows. Despite the tiny smudged prints of Jess's fingers, the coin was definitely gold. Grant looked at it and turned it over in his hand. He had seen these coins a million times and knew that it could have come from anywhere. The date of 1861 didn't help answer his questions. It was Federal issue, but that meant nothing. How could they tell the provenance of any one coin? Why date it? Money spent as easily on its first day as its twentieth year. The Southern coins had come from the Union. Fortunately for the Rebs, the coins had eagles imprinted on them, and not some leader of the Union. That might have proved embarrassing. Grant was glad, as he thought the practice of putting heroes on money was ludicrous.

Jesse leaned over and cupped a hand around Grant's ear. "Before you go making any brilliant deductions or deciding to keep that token, I put it down there for the boy to find. He was so fired up on digging for buried treasure. I couldn't bear to see him disappointed."

Grant nodded with a smile tucked in his beard. He had a soft spot for little Jess that would have made him do the same. He was glad to see that his father shared those feelings, even if it meant stashing coins for the boy to find.

Julia cleared her throat and held out the Bible. "We found this upstairs."

Jesse looked at her, and his mouth dropped open, causing his beard to hit his chest. "We relying on prayer now to find the money?" Grant knew that he'd never talk that way in the company of his wife, Hannah, who held staunch Methodist beliefs in the Almighty and His ways.

Julia shook her head and read the words from the book of St. Luke as she had done with her husband upstairs. "We found this passage marked in the book. It might be important. It certainly has to do with finding gold."

Newman nodded. "Well, I found this here key tied to the chandelier in the hallway." Grant looked down the hall and saw a smaller, cut-glass chandelier hanging in the distance. He didn't know if he would have noticed a key in the midst of the sparkling lights above his head. How had Newman managed to see the key when he needed to watch the floor and concentrate on getting around?

The large skeleton key looked to be gold-plated. It shone in the light and glistened with secrets. Grant took it from Newman's hand and studied it. He turned the key between his fingers.

The key might look good, but it had little use in a hamlet like Bethel. No one in a small town bothered to lock doors. The type of door that might be locked would need to be a secret door that hid behind a wall or inside a private house. The only way to find something like that would be going from house to house, and that was not even surefire. If the door were hidden, a cursory search wouldn't uncover it. With a large stash of gold, Woerner would be ingenious. Money was the mother of many inventions.

"So what now?" Jesse spoke the words that were on the mind of each person in the group. Just like him to do so.

Julia cleared her throat. "I'm still convinced that this passage has something to do with the gold. It's too coincidental not to be. We need to find some connection to linens or napkins."

Newman tapped one of his sticks on the floor. "Of course! I should have thought of that before."

"You know someone with a relationship to napkins?" Julia's cheeks had flushed slightly.

Grant worried that she had contracted the treasure-hunt spirit like everyone else in the room. Perhaps it had been best that she hadn't traveled to California with him, though he'd been miserably lonely. He'd seen too many folk consumed by gold fever there. He'd found other addictions out West.

"Micah Brown's woman makes lace. What do you call that?" Newman had beads of perspiration on his forehead, out of place on the late September day.

Grant wished that level heads would prevail, but the group seemed to be caught up in the hunt.

Julia practically beamed at her husband, looking full-faced at him and forgetting her lazy eye for a minute. "Tatting. That makes perfect sense."

This time no one spoke the obvious. Only Brown and Newman were left of the five original conspirators who had found the gold. If the agreement was that the last surviving member got the gold, one of the two of them was a killer. Grant looked at Newman and tried to see his youthful comrade as a murderer, but he couldn't do it. Still, that left Micah Brown, whom he'd also known. The easy way to find the killer might be to wait for the last man standing. Grant tried to look optimistic that he wouldn't lose all his chums to the temptation of easy money, but now he wasn't sure.

CHAPTER · 10

GRANT KNEW that he would never encourage Julia to take up a hobby after his visit to the Browns' home. Like his friends who had survived Andersonville, Micah Brown had somehow come up with the funds to build a minor mansion in Bethel, another two-story brick home at the corner of Water and Main. The home had high ceilings and walls of frosted glass. The fireplaces had been crowned with ceramic tiles and mirrors.

The thing that made the home unique, though, was the amount of lace used in the decorating. Grant had never seen as many doilies on a single sideboard as he did in the Brown home. From what he could see, they owned enough lace to cover the entire town in a frilly tent.

Grant was a plain man, a trait he'd inherited from his mother. Unless a body needed something to set a glass or a vase on, he saw no reason for doilies. Nobody, not even the White House with an ambassadorial reception for the civilized world, could need this number of dainty linens. If the parable were to be taken literally, the Browns' house would have been the source for the napkin to carry the gold.

Brown's wife was a heavyset woman, an imposing figure in a plain black dress. Grant had truly expected a lace collar on the garment, but she had refrained from her handiwork on her own person. Her faded red hair had been pulled up into a knot behind her head, and her face looked as if it had been pulled back along with the hair. Her cheeks were taut, and the corners of her mouth stretched out into a thin grim line. "General, how kind of you to pay a call on us."

Grant bowed at the waist and tipped his hat to the woman. "I'd be remiss in not seeing my old friends while I was in town. How are you, Mrs. Brown?"

She nodded to him. "Micah's in the next room. Let me go get him." She eyed the group of men who had accompanied him.

Newman had decided to listen in, and Jesse would never let a chance for thousands in gold slip through his grasp. The older Grant had carried a spring in his step since hearing about the treasure. He practically lived on Grant's coattails as if his son would lead him right to the gold.

Mrs. Brown came back into the room, followed by a skeleton of a man who had to be her husband. Had this not been their home, Grant wouldn't have recognized his one-time summer friend. He was a fraction of his former self. The Micah Brown of his youth had been a hearty boy with a smile and a quick joke. The man who entered the room had a scarecrow's build, few teeth, and less hair.

Grant knew that the prison camps had served raw pork and cornhusks for days on end, and that the men had suffered, but he hadn't seen anyone so gaunt before. The men at Andersonville had been moved from Belle Island. The earlier prison camp near Richmond had lost its rations as Grant's plan to burn out Virginia's breadbasket had begun to take hold. Is this what he'd done as a result of his strategy? He had no way to judge the difference a year in Andersonville could make. He felt a gut punch to think of his complicity in the matter.

Brown came forward and shook Grant's hand in a faint grip. "Sam, it's been a long time." The man's clasp felt as if he'd lost the battle with consumption or cholera. Death looked better than Brown.

"How you been, Micah?" Grant took a chair that his friend indicated with a crooked finger. For all his wife's busywork, Brown didn't look capable of picking up a doily, not to mention the tasks necessary to make one. Grant doubted that this man could have hauled gold from a wagon to a horse, much less the four hundred miles from Georgia.

Brown sat down in degrees like a slow-moving crick. He finally rested in the chair and looked across the room.

Grant had a sudden attack of conscience. How could he ask his friend to give up the money that sheltered him from the world now? Hadn't he suffered enough without being forced to make his way after his strength was gone? Wasn't he entitled to something?

Grant was lost in his thoughts and looked up to realize that Brown was deep into some story from the past. Jesse threw in a word now and then, a reminder to the man about what had happened. The main point of the story seemed to be Grant had tamed some horse after the creature had been called unbreakable. His ability to communicate on some level with the animals intrigued people who saw them as nothing more than a means to plow a field or to get from here to there.

Grant looked around, but Mrs. Brown had disappeared. Probably to tat a saddle for the 4th Ohio Cavalry. With her gone, Grant felt it easier to be forthright about the reasons for their visit. "Micah, you know that Woerner is dead. We're trying to find what he did with the gold."

Brown didn't speak. He sat ramrod stiff in the seat and swiveled his head to look at Grant and then Newman.

"Do you know what he did with it?" Jesse wasn't content to

be a spectator in any situation. The man forced himself onto the podium at rallies for his son and gave speeches hours longer than the guest of honor. Why would Grant expect him to be any less intrusive in his queries?

Brown shook his head. "I wasn't in much shape to carry gold. That is one heavy metal. Adam used to bring it to my house."

Grant shot a look at his father. He cleared his throat before resuming the conversation with Brown. "Well, we have reason to think that your wife might know more about the gold than she's telling."

Brown coughed, a racking croup that shook his entire body. The group waited for him to finish. "Nonsense. I'd know if Harriet knew anything."

Grant looked his friend in the eyes. "We're not saying she had something to do with the murders. We just found a clue that might suggest she knows where the gold is."

"Go ahead and ask." Brown unwound his stiff body enough to lean back in the chair. It pained Grant to see his friend move with such deliberate actions.

Mrs. Brown reentered the room without a summons from the group. Grant wondered where she had been that permitted her to hear the conversation so clearly. She stood next to her husband and draped a protective arm around his shoulder.

How much of the family work had she inherited since his return? Or while he was gone, for that matter? Grant was sure that the gold had made their lives easier. Money insulated people from the real world and the problems carried with the rough edges of everyday life.

"Ask me what?" Mrs. Brown's mouth didn't move as she spoke, making Grant wonder if indeed her hair was pulled too tight.

"Adam Woerner left a suggestion in his house that might

have a connection to you," Grant began. "Do you know anything about where he might have hidden the gold they found in Georgia?" He was almost embarrassed at the tenuous thread that connected the gold to Mrs. Brown. He would hate to explain the spider web of implications, broken with the slightest of breezes.

He wished Julia were here to deal with this woman. He trusted his wife to handle the fairer sex in almost all cases. Except for Mary Lincoln, Julia could handle most women with grace and aplomb. Certainly with more ease than he could.

Mrs. Brown held a hand to her bosom. "Me? Since when would Adam Woerner tell me about the gold? Why don't you ask Clarissa Halley? I'm sure he was much more likely to tell her about secret hiding places." She managed a little snort that reminded Grant that the Browns had once been pig farmers.

Newman sputtered and tried to intervene, but Jesse held him back. "Are you saying that Mrs. Halley and Adam Woerner were . . . involved?"

Grant knew what was underlying the words. If Halley's wife and Woerner were having relations, the motive for the crimes could be different. They'd all assumed that money bound the men, but illicit relationships would add too many permutations to contemplate.

Mrs. Brown merely sniffed at the question. She looked to her husband, who didn't utter a sound. From his furrowed brow and deep frown lines, he was obviously displeased that she had told tales out of school. Yet, he didn't speak against his wife.

From the sheer quantity of the lace, Grant was fairly certain he knew who ran the house. He could be no surer if Mrs. Brown had swaddled her husband in the material.

"Now, Harriet, Adam Woerner was over here a couple of months ago." Brown had turned to look at his wife and rested a hand on her arm.

"Not to talk about gold, he wasn't. He wanted me to show him how to make a lace pretty for his house." Her face lit up at the thought of tatting, and she started a long narrative of how she had gotten involved in the art.

Grant let her blather on for several minutes while the other men in the room looked as if a doctor had removed a lung without laudanum. He tried to think about other matters, but a few facts seeped in. She'd started tatting to while away the uncertain hours not knowing where her husband was after the Battle of Gettysburg. The tatting kept her company through the long years of his captivity, and finally she had started making some money at it in town to help support herself. Now she didn't need the money, but the hobby had become integral to her life. Their money had bought her some new equipment, and the house had a room devoted to lace and tatting now.

Mrs. Brown had just offered Grant a tour of the tatting room for a third time, when he decided to bring the conversation back to the topic at hand. He hoped by allowing the woman to talk about something she enjoyed that she would be more cooperative in helping them find the gold. "You mentioned that Woerner had come over to look at your lace. Was he interested in something particular?" Grant wondered if the man had a choice in listening to her talk about lace, or if he'd had an interest in something that might be related to the hiding place.

"Well, yes, he was. He had a particular pattern he wanted made for the top of his china hutch. It was a bit challenging, but he said I did it just fine." She beamed at the thought of a compliment on her work.

"When was this?" Grant took control. He wasn't sure if the men had deferred to his questions or if they had no idea where he was taking the line of inquiry.

"Well, it was right after the Fourth of July. He'd just had a party at his new home, and I remember that, because I knew the china hutch he was talking about. And I had to agree that a nice piece of lace would look lovely on it."

Grant decided that she would think that a coat rack would look good with a doily on it. Even so, he thought the timing was about right, though he doubted that Woerner truly gave a rat's patootie about doilies. Woerner could have made the lace as a clue to the hiding place of the gold, but Grant had no idea what the piece of lace could mean.

What was a man supposed to think about a doily? Woerner obviously wanted it to mean something, since he had marked that passage in the Bible, but who knew how the man's mind worked? Why couldn't they have given responsibility to someone who would write down the instructions on a piece of paper like a plain man would? Grant cursed Woerner and his fancy-thinking ways.

Jesse stood up and coughed. Apparently, he'd tolerated enough of the gentle arts for one morning.

Grant followed suit, and Brown led them to the door. Giving the general an enthusiastic but limp handshake, he said, "Curtis tried to escape and Collins wouldn't die, you know? That rope snapped and he fell to the ground like a sack of potatoes."

Newman looked at Grant and Jesse and explained, "He's talking about the Raiders. They were hung for their crimes against the other prisoners."

"You know they weren't buried with the rest of them." Brown's eyes had grown into the size of the double eagles, and he gripped Grant's hand in both of his. "That Wirz made them rot for eternity by themselves."

Grant furrowed his brow. He'd heard stories of men coming back from the war, not right in the head, but he'd not seen many of them. "So I heard, Micah. So I heard."

Brown's face relaxed into an easy smile. "Good to see you, Sam. Sorry about Harriet. She can prattle on for a time when you get her started."

Grant smiled at him. It was easy to be beneficent when he was leaving. "No problem. Julia can do the same at times."

Jesse made a face at his son as they left. He was not the type for niceties when they weren't required by social status. "Where to now?"

Grant pointed to the Woerner home. "Back to where we started today."

CHAPTER · 11

JULIA HELD UP the piece of linen and tried to decide which way was up. The tatted lace doily was square with a few random holes in it. "Ulys, what exactly is this pattern supposed to be? I've never seen a doily like this. They're usually flowers or snowflakes. This looks more like a hogweed."

Grant shrugged and spread a map out on the cornhusk mattress. "I have no idea. It must mean something, though. Woerner specifically asked Mrs. Brown to make it for him."

"Maybe he was just humoring a silly lady." Julia threw the doily on the washstand and approached her husband. She put a hand on his shoulder and leaned over to view the map. "And where did you find all this at? What makes you think this is important?"

He looked at her and smiled. "For starters, this was your idea. We followed the Bible story with the napkin to Mrs. Brown, who told us about the lace doily she made for Woerner. When we went back to Woerner's house this afternoon, we found it right where Mrs. Brown said it was. This map was underneath."

Julia looked at the square grid of Bethel again. "So this is what a treasure map looks like? I was expecting something more . . . thrilling."

Grant had to agree. He'd seen any number of maps like it during the war. The piece of paper held a surveyor's map of Bethel, complete with plat numbers and markings.

Little Jess bounded into the room. "Mr. Newman told me about the map." He lunged onto the bed and nearly crumpled the paper. "Can I see? Where's the X?"

Grant smoothed out the page again and pointed to the center of the map. "That's just the thing. I've found four marks on the page. It could be any of those places. I can't believe that Woerner went all over town to bury the stupid treasure, and then dug it all up on a monthly basis. It's not reasonable."

"Papa, where are they?" Little Jess could barely keep his skin on. The boy perched on the edge of the bed and swung his legs wildly. "When we going to go dig them up? I just know we're gonna find it."

"We can't just go digging up Bethel, Jess. People will talk and wonder what is going on. A certain amount of discretion is needed over a campaign like this. The whole town can't see us look for gold. Before you know it, everyone and their grandmother will be digging up the street corner with a spade." Grant began to fold the map back up.

For all his work with maps and cartography during the war, he couldn't divine much from this particular specimen. The map was definitely Bethel—that much was easy to see. Otherwise, it looked like an ordinary surveyor's map. A few places on the map had been marked with a pen, but Grant had expected a more dramatic signpost to a fortune in coins. Instead, four small X's had been marked on the page, and Grant couldn't see that any one of them looked more promising than the others.

He recollected the time that Woerner had hid a frog in his sister's bathwater. He was like that. He no doubt was having a good chuckle, wherever he was, watching these simple folk try to cipher out what he'd left for them.

Even with the chance that the doily meant nothing, Grant had taken it and the map from Woerner's home. The other men had a glazed look of greed in their eyes when they discovered the doily map. Grant relied more on Julia's good sense than the likes of his father's get-rich-quick schemes. Jesse would find a way to take the map to market and sell it to the highest bidder.

Grant didn't like the map, though. He was distrustful of things that seemed too easy, and leaving a map out in a house for anyone to find seemed just that simple. Woerner had a twisted mind, one that liked to make people think one thing while he did another. Marking the gold on a surveyor's map seemed too straightforward for his tastes.

Still, no one else would be satisfied with Grant's conclusions. With so much money at stake, everyone would insist on trying every tack possible. That would mean digging in one or more of the sites on the map before they would concede that he was right. He was willing to bide his time, provided that the killer was as well. If the murderer struck again, Grant would have to find another path to solve this matter. Or he could just settle on the last man standing.

He finally chose the site at Main and Circus for the group's first dig. The name seemed telling, since the search had taken on some of those characteristics. Plus the spot had the distinction of being the farthest from the center of town. However, Grant held few illusions that everyone in the hamlet wouldn't know exactly what was happening before the group could wash the mud from their shoes.

Jess had already pulled digging instruments from Newman's root cellar before the rest of the family made it downstairs. The boy had no end of energy when it came to something exciting—when it came to tasks he wanted to do. Chores and errands seemed to induce his lethargy. Still, Grant didn't mind. Nell was already wanting to spend more time with her school friends and less time with the family. Soon she'd be lost to her pa. Jess was the last Grant child at home, and the general wanted to enjoy every minute of the boy.

The group had gathered in the kitchen before making their way out of the house like a well-trained army regiment. Julia, who had insisted on going along, carried the map and walked beside her husband, commenting on the changes in the town since she'd been there for Buck's birth, some thirteen years earlier. It seemed to Grant like a lifetime since he had been on the West Coast and his bride had come to stay in Bethel, but it hadn't been all that many years since he'd been an unhappy captain in the Army. Now he was the general for the Federal Army, leading a wild-goose chase across the streets of an Ohio town.

He certainly had taken a step down from leading the Union Army to organizing a treasure hunt in a country village. He wasn't sure what Stanton or Seward would say if they were to see this fool's parade. They held their Cabinet positions in high regard. Of course, they might be more forgiving if they knew this spectacle could help pay down the war debt.

The small troop arrived at the designated spot on the map. For a few minutes, Grant thought that perhaps the others had a good idea. The corner was an empty lot, a bare patch of dying hogweed and grass. A grove of locust trees made it a shady quarter acre. The lot wasn't fenced in.

The others quickly set upon the spot. Jess let out a whoop when he found a small marker. A stone obelisk, no more than eighteen inches high and shaped liked the unfinished Washington monument in the capital, sat towards one edge of the lot.

Grant inspected the marker and found that it wasn't very

old. It was conceivable that Woerner had installed it recently to mark the gold's location, but Grant had his doubts. It looked more like a touch point, an arrow to something bigger and more important. Yet the stone block gave up no secrets.

Grant still couldn't believe the plan's simplicity. The map seemed too easy, too fortuitous. No one would hide thousands of dollars in gold coins under a visible marker, even if it was in a small town. The temptation was too great.

Jess laid into the ground with a pickax. He took a few good swings before his grandfather joined him. Newman pulled up the marker and carefully rested it on the side of Circus Street. The tufts of grass that had survived the first killing frosts were the only things distinguishing property from street.

The namesake Grants were already a foot into the ground and still swinging. Jess had managed to get most of the fill from the hole on his clothes. He already had streaks of mud on his cheeks and brow. Grant was amazed at how dirt seemed to attract children like a magnet.

Jesse fared a bit better. He'd rested his coat on a locust tree branch stretching over the lot and rolled up his sleeves. Grant's father was definitely not afraid of hard work if it was profitable. The man had spent his early years in little more than indentured labor until he could become a tanner. Grant recalled his own childhood with the days of tanning leather, where the house and yard stunk of entrails and rotting carcasses. Digging a few feet into the ground wasn't much for a man who could skin an animal without flinching.

Grant hated to tell the pair that he suspected nothing was buried there. He thought back to the funeral he had attended two days earlier for Christopher Halley. The ground on top of the gravesite was freshly turned and damp. He didn't see any signs of disturbed earth here. The ground was packed hard, and grass grew in fits and starts all over the lot. No indication that

Woerner had dug up a treasure anytime recently.

Newman stood next to Julia, who seemed to view the outing as a working picnic. She'd brought odds and ends to eat and a blanket that she had rested about twenty yards from the digging. She carefully spread out the blanket and set down a basket of snacks for the group. She felt much the same way about Jess that her husband did. Allow him some freedom to be a child—and treasure hunts were the centerpiece to any boy's vivid imagination.

Maybe that excitement as well as greed lured men with its siren song, Grant thought. It was no different from the romantic notions that men held about warfare. Many a man in the North had signed up for war thinking of the grandeur and the exhilaration of traveling and battling the enemy. Now they'd come home, starved to skeletons and missing limbs. Was combat still so exciting to those young men?

Jesse and his grandson had now dug about two feet. The boy had climbed down into the hole to get a better shot at hitting something, but so far the thick Ohio clay was the only pay dirt they'd found. Jesse threw another clump of clay behind him and stopped to wipe his brow. He looked at the picnickers with disgust. "Why aren't you over here helping, Ulysses? Those men were your friends."

Grant frowned. Finding the gold wasn't the same as finding the person responsible for his friends' deaths. The material profit that Jesse had in mind was unrelated to the murders at hand. If they found the Confederate gold, Jesse would be just as happy to move on to Cincinnati and forget the men who had died on its altar.

By this point, the pair had dug down almost three feet and had found nothing more interesting than a few old Indian arrowheads. Jess wasn't in the mood to look at them now, but Grant pulled them from the clumps of dirt and scraped them clean. The boy would probably want to see them when his fancy turned from pirates to the Far West again.

Grant wanted to stop, but he didn't know of a good way to demand that they abandon their quest. Other than mussing up someone's unused property, they weren't causing any harm. No one in town would question him; he commanded too much respect for saving the Union for someone to demand to know why his family was intent on digging a hole in an empty lot.

Grant tipped his hat to a woman as she strolled past with her toddler. The little one looked fascinated by the scene and wanted to play in the dirt. Just like a child. The woman looked slightly shocked as if she'd never seen men working.

Jesse had finally gotten the hint and started digging in a different location. Newman stood by watching the pair dig and offered suggestions. With only one leg, he couldn't be of much help to them in the way of labor, but he pointed to spots where any treasure might be.

Jesse dug down a few feet at the new location and stopped to mop his brow. Despite the cool temperature, the group had worked up a sweat in trying to find the gold. Little Jess ran over to the blanket, threatening his mother with filthy hands.

Julia wiped him off as best she could and handed him some apple cider. Fall meant the harvest of the best apples in town, and the Fagleys of Bethel still had the most delicious orchards in Ohio. Robert Simpson, Grant's cousin, had married into the apple family. Grant loved the taste of the red ripe apples that came from their land.

The group seemed quieter now than when they had begun. Grant was glad that he'd let them dig. He would never have heard of the end of it if he hadn't, but he knew that Woerner wouldn't make it so easy for anyone to find the gold. The boy had been cunning in his youth, and Grant didn't believe for a minute that Andersonville had changed him that drastically. He would never have left the treasure out in an open lot to be found by anyone. Besides, the empty parcel of land didn't explain the key that Newman had found. It meant something.

People didn't lock up very much in a town like Bethel. You knew your neighbors and your friends. You trusted them. Maybe that's why it was so easy for someone to kill three men. Who would suspect the men you'd grown up with and fought alongside of? You'd had a common enemy then, and now the killer was one of you. All for gold.

After digging for a while, and dejected by the lack of success, the group gave up and marched back to Newman's. Jesse dragged the shovel behind him and handed it to Grant before heading back towards his temporary lodging. The group entered Newman's house. Patsy announced that she had heated water for baths after the dirty outing. Grant looked at her with gratitude. He wondered where Newman had found help like this; she obviously knew her way around children. She escorted Jess off to the tub as Julia went upstairs to rest.

CHAPTER · 12

THE SCENE IN THE BEDROOM could have been from a Currier and Ives lithograph had the topic of conversation not been stolen goods and murder. Julia sat on the edge of the cornhusk mattress, splitting her gaze between her husband and the map of Bethel. Grant took his time spreading out the map on the home-stitched quilt and puzzled over where a treasure could be in Southern Ohio. The couple had their heads close to one another, and he had his arm around her waist.

Julia took a long look at the map on the bed and then turned to the Bible that she'd placed on the dresser. "Ulys, maybe we've been looking at this the wrong way."

Grant looked up from the map and smiled. "Obviously we have, or we'd have found the gold this afternoon and Jess wouldn't be quite so muddy."

Julia tittered and reached out for the map. She started folding it into sections as she spoke. "No, I meant that we should be concentrating on the murders and not on the money. People matter most. If we find out who is killing the veterans, then we should be able to locate the gold."

He stared off into space as he pondered her words. Julia knew what she was talking about. She understood people and had an uncanny knack for knowing things without being told. "You may be right. The two have to be related somehow."

She finished folding the map back up and smiled at Grant as she handed it back to him. "There are so many things we could look into. And we don't have to get filthy."

Grant laughed, knowing that keeping her petticoats pristine was behind his wife's sudden compassion. Just like Julia to worry about making a proper presentation of herself. "I've been meaning to talk to the doctor about Halley," he said. "See if he thinks it could have been poison that killed him."

Julia smiled. "Well, of course, that would have to be Dr. Peck, the man who helped deliver Buck. We could call on him together."

Grant smiled. He took pleasure in the way that Julia insinuated herself into these situations. Much as he enjoyed her companionship, he worried that she might be in danger. His work often put her in harm's way. He'd worried about her during the war, being too close to the front line. Yet she had never seemed to mind. "Well, it's a mite late now to be paying social calls," he said.

Julia slid her arm through his and pulled him a bit closer. "Then, General, we shall do it tomorrow."

True to her word, Julia dressed for a social visit the next morning. She didn't neglect to bring several pictures of Buck, their second son, with her as the couple walked down Main Street. Grant was glad to have her along. His wife could coerce any conversation around to the subject she desired. Usually it had to do with her social standing or her husband's military rank, but it came in handy with country gossip, as well.

The doctor had his office in his house. Unlike the homes Grant had seen so far in Bethel, this homestead would be considered modest. The clapboard house was one level, with no porch or dramatic entryway. Dr. Peck answered his own door and greeted Julia warmly.

Grant had been in the Washington Territory at Fort Vancouver when Buck was born and hadn't been introduced to his son for over two years. He'd dearly missed the time with his babies. Dr. Peck was a relative stranger, a man Grant had met on a few social calls, but who had played a profound role in his family. He had never heard much about the doctor from Julia in her infrequent correspondence. Of course, one letter every six months left a lot to the imagination.

Dr. Peck smiled as Julia showed him the photographs of their son. Buck was thirteen now and more like his father all the time, or so people told Grant. The boy had been named Ulysses S. Grant, Jr., even though that wasn't Grant's birth name. The lad had not lived long with the moniker, though. Since he'd been birthed in Ohio, people called him Buck, for the Buckeye boy. The name stuck despite Julia's best efforts to remedy the situation.

Dr. Peck shook Grant's hand and invited the couple inside. The waiting area of the dispensary was empty, and the only sound was the ticking clock. *The town must be suffering from an outbreak of health*, Grant thought. The doctor led them into a large airy room that held a different style of love seat along each wall. Two filing cabinets, a desk, and a chair staked out the middle of the room.

The files caught Grant's interest. Halley's records would most likely be stored there with details about the rest of the soldiers who had passed. Sadly, no medical records could tell if Woerner had died of a simple fall or of murder. Science would never be that precise.

Dr. Peck went to check on tea, the only offered libation, and left the couple in the waiting area. Grant debated about rummaging through the medical records while the sawbones was gone, but he thought better of it. If this visit was supposed to be under the guise of a social call, snooping would be out of the question.

The doctor returned with tea after a few minutes and served his guests in silence. After the advantage of a servant for the past few months, Grant was humbled to remember that he was more accustomed to these circumstances than serving help. He took his tea and swallowed a mouthful. He wished that the doctor would have offered him something stronger, but with a lady present, that was unlikely. Grant looked around for an ash-can or spittoon, but those were not present. Apparently, the doctor practiced the life he preached.

Presently, after Julia had spent a good twenty minutes talking about Buck and Nell to the doctor, she mentioned the Halleys. Grant's ears perked up as he heard the name, and he set the teacup down on the end table next to the love seat on which they sat. The doctor certainly couldn't suspect the real purpose of their visit.

"We were supposed to stay with the Halleys. The general knew Mr. Halley from their younger days. The general used to visit during summers at West Point." Julia made it a point of calling Grant by his title in front of company. As if anyone could have missed the events of the past four years and the role Grant played in shaping national history.

"Aah, yes. The Halleys." The doctor scratched his long whiskers and looked at the pair. Grant knew that something was wrong. Dr. Peck's gaze bounced back from one to the other, as if he were trying to size up the couple.

Grant's quiet countenance exuded reliability and sturdiness. If he couldn't get the doctor to talk, no one could.

Julia turned her eyes down in an uncharacteristically demure pose. "Did I say something wrong, Doctor?"

The doctor turned chivalrous and harrumphed a few times

for good show. "Not at all, my dear lady. Not at all. I just wasn't sure what to say about the situation at the Halley home."

Julia looked to her husband and gave a smile that spoke volumes. They had been married long enough for Grant to know exactly what each of her expressions meant. She had conquered the doctor thoroughly and knew that it was merely a matter of time before she got the desired information.

"You can count on us to keep quiet," she said. "We're not staying with Mrs. Halley. We really don't know the widow all that well."

Grant knew what Julia was saying: *We don't know her, so tell us everything you can.*

The doctor made a noise in his throat that Grant thought should be checked out with a tongue depressor. "I'm glad to hear that. She might be having some difficult times coming up."

She arched her well-plucked eyebrows. Grant loved to watch his wife operate on small-town men in the same way that she handled Washington diplomats and ambassadors. "Difficult?" Julia's genteel upbringing allowed her to wield her honed etiquette like a bayonet. She knew the appropriate mix of iron and velvet to use.

The doctor looked at her and almost seemed to forget that Grant was in the room. "Well, it's not pleasant, but Mr. Halley's mother has made some rather nasty statements. I'm not sure how to handle them. I certainly don't know that anything could be proved, but I hate to see someone mired in accusations."

Julia put a small hand to her throat, brushing the cameo around her neck. "I don't understand you. What statements are you talking about?"

The doctor smiled and patted her free hand. Grant knew that he had years of bedside manner in treating the biddies in town. He wondered if the doctor had ever met anyone of Julia's natural guile.

"Some people are saying that Mrs. Halley expedited her husband's departure from this earth. I have no idea what means they are suggesting she used."

"People are saying that about her?" Julia feigned surprise. To Grant, the scene was as obvious as a horse pie on a summer day, but the doctor seemed to be taken in. "Could it be true?" she asked.

The doctor nodded. "I probably shouldn't tell you this, but we may never know how many people die from poisons. There's no way to tell. General, it's a good thing that you seem to have the devotion of your wife. So many men could be slaughtered in that manner."

Grant decided to chime in. "So it could have been murder and no one would be the wiser."

The doctor squirmed in his chair. "Well, I didn't think so at the time. I must say that Halley had been a very sick man. He came back from Georgia emaciated, little more than a bag of bones. I helped nurse him back to health, but the prison camp fare had ruined his digestive tract. He had a very limited diet without much nutritious value to it. So it could have been natural causes. The coroner, Dr. Shroen, backed me up on the diagnosis."

Neither Grant nor Julia spoke. They let Dr. Peck proceed at his own pace in the telling.

"In retrospect, though, it could have been poison. The symptoms could have been arsenic, but it's a difficult call without more suspicions than I had. The poison closely mimics gastritis."

"Did he have a special diet? I would assume his food would have to be bland." Julia talked about the kitchen as if she were in one every day.

"Yes, so it's unlikely that anyone else would eat his portions. So a person could conceivably put something in his meal without fear of tainting anyone else in the household."

"So no one would be the wiser if Mrs. Halley had slipped some poison into the poor man's food? It all sounds too easy."

The doctor shook his head. "Not in this case. Halley died rather suddenly. If a person was trying to surreptitiously murder someone, they wouldn't administer the poison to him all in one dose. They would dole it out over time, allowing the poison to build up in the system. The symptoms would be a matter of degrees, and most medical men would never even know the difference. Mrs. Halley never struck me as a stupid woman, and poisoning in a single dose would be dangerous at best. People talk."

"But she got away with it." Julia had a glint in her eye. Grant wondered what thought had crossed her mind. She often claimed to have a psychic sense, and Grant had rarely found her intuition to be wrong. Her ideas would be worth pursuing.

"Did she?" The doctor looked slightly chagrined at his former patient's macabre curiosity. He probably wasn't used to a woman like Julia, who spoke her mind and knew her course. "Many of the people in town are tattling about Halley's death. Why, I was at the services at the Methodist church the other night, and people were clucking about it openly. Dr. Shroen's and my conclusions seem to mean nothing to these people."

Grant wondered what Reverend Evans would say about the rumors. After all, he could hardly bite the hand that fed him so well. New steeples and bells didn't come without a price, and Mrs. Halley had been a generous donor. Yet several commandments had been trampled in the previous few days. How could the preacher countenance these matters, regardless of the personal cost?

How would the sheriff handle a death where the authorities said no crime had been committed? He might leave it alone for a while, but eventually the lawman would be forced to act.

"Was Mr. Halley . . . difficult? Would she be better off without him?" Julia looked directly at the doctor.

"I never found him to be cross, but it's hard to know what goes on behind closed doors. My, how did we ever get onto this topic? Not exactly the best thing to talk about when one of my favorite patients comes to call."

Julia took that as a dismissal and rose from the seat. "It's been so good to see you, Doctor. I'll make sure to tell Buck and Nellie that we saw you again. They'll be happy to know."

Grant rose with his wife and shook the doctor's hand. It felt strange to think that this man had a larger role than his own in his son's formative first two years. Grant had been alone and miserable without his family in California. He'd drunk to mask his misery and finally resigned his commission to be by their side again. Ironically, old Jeff Davis had approved his resignation. Funny how time had a way of changing roles.

Dr. Peck followed the Grants to the door and let them out. Grant could have sworn that the doctor's eyes followed them until they were well on their way back to Newman's house.

Chapter · 13

WHEN GRANT AWOKE the following morning, he was alone. Julia was gone, as was little Jess. He thought about luxuriating in bed for a few hours, a rare treat for someone long used to army cots and the hard Virginia earth, but he decided to see if he could find his host instead.

Newman had been missing when they returned the night before. Perhaps Julia was asking him about Mrs. Halley and the suspicions that surrounded her murdering her husband. Newman already knew Julia's obloquy regarding Mrs. Halley, so he was the logical person to discuss the matter with.

Since Grant couldn't find any trace of his host, he was tempted momentarily to search for clues. The two surviving men were the most likely suspects in any killings, as the number of likely candidates was dwindling rapidly. If the gunshot was related to the gold—and he had every reason to think it was—then either Newman was innocent or he had an accomplice. Grant knew of no way to fire a rifle without your finger on the trigger. There was no way to shoot from a distance. The recoil of a gun was more than a match for Micah Brown, who would tip over in a breeze. He was more likely to fit in a rifle barrel, rather than fire one.

Grant heard noises from the kitchen and made his way to the back of the home. The aroma of coffee told him that Patsy was still at the house. His impromptu search would have to be postponed. She would have no reason to keep Grant's treacheries against his host to herself.

"Morning, General. Mr. Newman told me that you should makes yourself at home. He had to go fetch some things from his cousins out near Felicity."

Grant nodded. A trip to the small town in the next county meant that Newman would be gone several hours. Of course, Grant still didn't know where Julia had got off to. She could be visiting any one of a number of people in town, for who-knows-what nefarious purposes. She owed a visit to his mother's family, the Simpsons, as well as some of Jesse's friends who had helped her during her pregnancies.

Without asking, Patsy slid a plate down on the table in front of Grant. He was used to fending for himself, even as he'd risen in the ranks. His aide, Major Rawlins, might lecture him on the evils of the demon alcohol and act like a mother hen at times, but he would never dream of serving breakfast to the general. Patsy poured him a cup of coffee and set it in front of the plate, which held hog jowl bacon and a sausage link as thick as the woman's arm.

Grant dug in, and she seemed content not to speak as she performed the chores around the kitchen. He was almost finished when Julia returned, poking her head in the kitchen. "Morn', Ulys. How are you today?"

He nodded, not wanting to risk a lecture on speaking with his mouth full. When Julia was in a maternal mode, she corrected everything the family did, himself included.

"Well, I went to visit the Simpsons this morning," she said. "I thought I might be able to confirm a few of the musings of the doctor yesterday."

Grant jerked his head in Patsy's direction. Julia was used to her own servants, who had been with her for years. Those folk could be trusted with the Confederate gold if necessary. That bond made her complacent about talking in front of other people's help, as if they could share the same level of honor. Grant didn't know Patsy's antecedents, but he was sure she would owe more loyalty to her employer than to the Grants. She'd know on which side her bread was buttered.

"Well, we can take a walk in a few minutes and I'll tell you everything." Julia hummed a few bars of a war song, and Grant wondered why that tune had popped into her head. She seemed peculiarly buoyed, and Grant had no idea why. The bed was warm and comfortable, but that certainly couldn't explain the morning's smiles and songs.

Grant mopped up the gravy on his plate with the remnants of a biscuit and followed after his wife. A morning constitutional would be good for him anyway. The rich meals and more sedentary life had made his uniforms fit a bit tighter these days. His 5'8" frame didn't allow room for extra weight.

They were a solid two blocks from the Newman house before Julia began her story. "Well, Ulys, it does seem like our near hostess has been a busy woman."

The devil is no match for a clever woman, Grant thought. His wife was twice the spy that Rose Greenhow was. He shivered remembering that she'd drowned, weighed down by gold coins sewn into her clothing.

"Do tell. It seems like you've been busy as well."

Julia sputtered for a second and tapped Grant's arm in a mock fashion. "You're in spirits today. You know precisely what I mean."

"So how are the Simpsons, dear wife? I'm sure they bore more news than just the antics of Mrs. Halley." The couple continued walking along Plane Street.

Julia filled a few blocks of town with the gossip regarding her in-laws. Apparently from the amount of information that Julia had gleaned in such a short time, the rest of the Simpsons were nothing like his own taciturn mother. They must practically prattle on like old hens: who was married, who had died, and who was with child. All of the things that made this country move on after the war and continue on its great path.

Grant hoped that in a few years, the circle of life and death would make people forget and forgive some of the transgressions of the previous four years. He wanted the Union to adopt a spirit of forgiveness and tolerance. The country should reunite and heal. Even his cousin Robert Simpson was doing better after bouts of ill health at the end of the war. However, it would be a few months before he was well enough to farm again.

They were almost to the skirts of Bethel, which was only about five blocks from the hamlet's center, when Julia finished the Simpson tales. Grant would need to remember all of the stories for his mother's benefit when they reached Covington. She would expect him to know the entire family tree's current situation, like a school examination. Hannah reminded him of Julia in their mutual devotion to family, though in his mother's case, it was rarely expressed verbally.

"So what are these things that you heard? I've been waiting patiently." Grant turned them right on West Street. The town of Bethel was built on a grid of square blocks that made navigation simple. They could ring the town by going from West Street to North to East and then South Street. The planners had designed the layout to be relatively easy in style and in form.

They continued on past Osborn Street as a steady wind pushed at their backs. A few dead leaves swirled at their feet. "Well, from what I was told, the widow Halley wasted no time in finding a new beau. In fact, some of your relatives speculated that perchance she had started courting before Mr. Halley was dead."

Grant blushed a little. Despite the women of easy virtue who had hung around his camps for years, he still tried to think of women as dainty, proprietous creatures, not harlots who kept a line of men on a string. He had hoped Halley's last days on earth had been good ones. Now he questioned whether they had been.

"Your family goes to the same Methodist Episcopal church as the Halleys," she continued. "They knew them socially. Mrs. Halley was accustomed to being on her own while her husband was in prisoner of war camp. Not that there were any eligible men left in town. All the menfolk were off fighting. It was very difficult for her to get used to having him home again."

He nodded. The story made sense. He'd heard similar stories from other enlisted men. Fortunately, Grant had learned his lessons during the California years. He'd been miserable without his wife. Those long lonely months alone drove him to drink. Julia was a poor correspondent. He'd gone months without a letter, having no way of knowing when Buck had been born and if the baby was a boy or a girl.

By the time that the war started in 1861, he knew that Julia had to accompany him, if he were to fight effectively. With a few rare exceptions, she followed him through the campaigns of the war. On occasion, she'd nearly been captured, but nothing replaced the joy of having her at his side. She brought the children as well, likening their education on the battlefields if not in schools, as that of Alexander the Great learning at the feet of Philip of Macedonia. She was not above hyperbole when it came to his career.

Even though women were the weaker sex and prone to emotions, Grant carried no sympathy for adulterers. Men were expected to use self-control. Absence might make the heart grow fonder, but it was no excuse for women to stray. He knew that it happened, even as he knew that he could never so cruelly betray his beloved. "So who was the shameful man who took advantage of the woman?"

Julia walked ahead of her husband a few steps. Grant knew that she didn't want to tell him this part—it would upset him. By walking ahead, she didn't have to look him in the eye as she told him. "Well, at first, it was a merchant who was traveling through town, but since the war, she's been spending a great deal of time with our Mr. Newman."

Grant sputtered. "Zeke Newman? I don't believe it."

"I didn't think you would, but the Simpsons were adamant. She sneaks over to his house using backyards so as not to be seen. Of course, she *was* seen, and it looks much worse when you skulk—like you have something to hide." Julia maintained her pace so she wouldn't have to look at him. Grant tried to speed up, but she seemed to know his tactics without watching him.

Grant remembered seeing Mrs. Halley at the Newman house a few days earlier. At the time, he hadn't been sure. It hadn't made sense for her to run to Newman, but if they were having an affair, maybe she felt a need to check what he was going to tell Grant. By telling identical stories, less doubt would be cast on their version of the truth. He had questioned his eyes that day, but now he was certain that she'd hurried over to see Newman. That didn't look good for the couple if they were cheating.

They turned on to North Street. At least the wind no longer pushed them forward. Grant remained in silence for a few minutes, mulling over what Julia had related. He'd have to talk to Newman about this, host or no host. He wasn't sure he countenanced having little Jess in an adulterous house. If the pair was involved, then their actions would have to be more carefully explored.

Grant wondered why Julia continued to walk a few paces ahead, until she cleared her throat to speak again. "Well, the past few weeks, she and Mr. Newman were no longer involved. Several people were shocked to find out that she'd been spending time with Adam Woerner."

Grant let out a groan. It was one thing to have two viable suspects because of an affair, but this woman seemed determined to implicate every last conspirator in her adultery. The motives became endless. Especially when her last lover was the most recent victim.

"Oh, I know. It's shocking, but Robert said that he saw her go to Mr. Woerner's place on more than one occasion. Unaccompanied." Julia said the word like it was a verdict of guilt, rather than merely suggestive.

With thousands in gold floating around Bethel, Grant had to wonder if perhaps Mrs. Halley was blackmailing Woerner. With so much money at stake, it seemed more likely. If someone had murdered her husband, she lost the generous monthly allowance that the gold afforded her. In order to maintain the well-kept life she'd grown used to, it made sense to pursue another member of the same group.

Woerner was a bachelor with an eye for the ladies. When Grant was at West Point, he had heard the rumors about how Woerner got a local girl in trouble. She'd been shipped off to a home for unwed mothers in a flurry of scandal. Nothing untold had happened to Woerner. No condemnation and no reproach. Grant had no doubt that he'd been the same type of man until he died.

Men didn't change over the years. Bobby Lee never got a demerit at West Point, and he'd turned into a man who'd prided himself on protocol and manners. No matter that he'd fought to keep men in captivity.

"Ulys, what if we've been looking at this matter all wrong? What if these deaths have nothing to do with the gold? There are other human motivators besides greed. Love, jealousy, revenge."

Grant nodded. He'd been lost in the same thoughts. He was glad to have Julia along on this trip. He needed her constant counsel and advice. "Well, I have given that some thought," he exaggerated. "No one came looking for the map after Woerner's death. If the money was the motive, I would have thought that the killer would have searched high and low for it. The gold doesn't benefit anyone if it's lost."

"Indeed. Well, that's a worry. What if the killer comes after us to get the map? What should we do?"

Grant scoffed. "Give it to him. I haven't as much as made an attempt to hide it yet. So it should be easy to find. Besides, except for that blamed key, no one locks a thing in this town."

Julia slowed down enough to touch Grant's arm and look at him. "Ulys, what if the killer doesn't have to fetch the map?"

He squinted and tried to follow where this path was going. At last check, the map was still in their room. "You mean like a copy of it or something?"

She shook her head and made a small shiver. "No, what if the killer is Mr. Newman. He's been with us every step of the way. He has as much access to it now as if he had it in his pocket."

Grant paused for a second. Julia was right. If Newman had killed those men, not only was he in line to collect the gold, he was also in line to inherit Mrs. Halley as well. Grant didn't like the thought, but it had merit. There were only a few people who could benefit from the deaths. Newman was at the top of the list. Perhaps he'd enlisted an accomplice to take a shot at them. After all, it had missed. And Grant had allowed his family to be taken in by him.

CHAPTER · 14

GRANT DIDN'T KNOW the proper etiquette for accusing his host of theft, adultery, and murder. He decided to give it a bit of time, hoping that an opening in the conversation might allow the subject to be broached. He wasn't sure that accusations of breaking multiple commandments cropped up at the dinner table very often.

As it turned out, Grant didn't have long to wait. He sat in the parlor with Julia and little Jess. His son yearned to divine other places to dig in town. The boy had managed to trace lines across the map, connecting the four points that had been marked. The lines intersected, and Jess was fervently trying to convince his father to dig for more treasure at that location the following morning.

Newman came quietly into the room. He smiled to watch the boy play with the map and try to determine what existed at the site marked by the intersection.

When Jess discovered that one of the points was the Methodist Episcopal church, he decided that perhaps another tack was needed. He started studying the points again, trying to arrive at a combination that would lead to gold. Fortunately, he treated the matter like one of his penny novels and didn't seem to realize that at least two men had died for the treasure so far.

Grant was well aware of the dangers involved. He didn't put much faith in his son's daydreams. He doubted that any adult would feel threatened by Jess's vivid attempts to hunt down the gold. As yet, no one had shown interest in the map. Either the killer knew where the gold was or he bode his time to retrieve the map.

Grant didn't notice Newman at first, until the man sat down in an empty horsehair seat. He looked tired, and Grant wondered if he'd been having trouble sleeping. With all the activities he and Julia suspected their host of, Newman should be nigh exhausted.

"Sam, I've been thinking about what you said yesterday, and I just don't see how it could have happened."

Julia got up, leaned down next to Jess, and helped him gather up the map and pencils. They left without a word, but the look in Julia's eyes meant that she would be told everything at a later moment.

"You're referring to Halley's death?"

Newman nodded. "Clarissa loved Chris. I don't see how you can think that she killed him in cold blood."

Grant tugged on his beard for a second. Despite his desire to talk to Newman about the subject, he hadn't expected the man to give him such wide latitude in bringing it up. Still, it was rather natural. The intervening decades had narrowed their topics of conversation. This type of activity was bound to get some jawing. Murder didn't happen very often in a small town.

Milking cows and raising tobacco had to be dull in comparison to four years of bullets whistling past your head. Grant found himself missing the command of men, though not battle and bloodshed. "Well, I do know that the doctor isn't quite sure now of his diagnosis. Apparently people are talking that Mrs.

Halley killed her husband. They expect Dr. Peck to do something about it."

Newman averted his gaze, pretending to be fascinated by the floor. "There's nothing they can really do about it, is there? I mean, can they prove poison?"

Grant sputtered for a moment. He hadn't mentioned poison, nor had he told his friend that there was no way to determine if some fatal drug had been administered. He wondered again if Newman had been confabulating with Mrs. Halley about these matters. "Well, technically, no. But you know the saying: Where there's smoke. . . ."

"There's a bunch of old gossipy clucks. That's all I know."

Grant decided to lead with a forward charge, the best method in his eyes. He wasn't big on looking back. "Those same old hens are saying that you have something going on with Mrs. Halley. That's the reason why people are speculating about murder."

Using just his arms, Newman raised himself up out of his chair. He stood there without his sticks, one leg holding him upright. Without assistance, the missing leg was that much more noticeable. His fists clenched into balls. "Who's been saying that? I've done nothing wrong with her. Nothing."

Grant patted his friend on the arm and felt the hard sinewy muscles in his biceps. If someone was going to dig for that treasure, Newman, with his arms built up from crutching, would be an ideal choice. Grant wondered if perhaps he had already indulged in some searching on his own. Even if he had, Newman hadn't shown any signs of helping when the troop had dug out on Circus Street. He'd looked as though he wasn't capable. "I'm not saying you did, but I did see Mrs. Halley over here one day. She actually came through the backyard, if I got the logistics correct. That can look a mite sneaky."

Newman sighed and sat back down. "Well, she's been helping me—with a personal problem. That's all. It's easier to go to the back door in this place. It's so big that sometimes Patsy doesn't hear folks at the front. So Clarissa goes to the back door to make sure that Patsy answers."

Grant nodded and tried to look sanguine. Of course, Newman would have pat answers to the questions, and if he had any sense, he knew that people would talk. It was natural. Yet his reaction to the gossip seemed real—and intense. It still pained Grant to read the accounts in the newspapers of his own deeds, most pure calumny. Newman had it easy.

Grant cleared his throat to give himself a chance to think. He didn't want to offend the man who had shown them kindness when the Halleys were grieving, but at the same time, the rumors were difficult to ignore, especially if they led to murder. "Well, there's also been talk about Adam Woerner and Mrs. Halley as well. People seem to think that she threw you over for him."

Newman barked out a hoarse laugh. The sound brought Patsy from the kitchen, wiping her hands on her apron as she stepped into the room. "Is everything okay?"

She let the apron fall and patted it back into place. Newman stood up again and let her have his seat. He moved to the love seat next to the chair and sat down awkwardly. "General Grant here seems to think that Mrs. Halley and I are having an affair."

Patsy put a gnarled hand to her mouth and tittered. "Oh, I see. My, my."

Newman reached out a hand and patted the woman on the knee. "I think it's best that I tell him."

Patsy frowned for a second, her eyes narrowing with some emotion. The expression cut deep lines across her face that told Grant she was older than he first thought, maybe ten years older than his own age. She was fifty if she was a day.

Newman smiled at Grant, then looked down at his one leg. He began to speak, and Grant wished he could see what emotions were running through the man's eyes. "Clarissa and I are not having an affair. Patsy and I are courting."

Grant was glad for the cover of his beard. Otherwise, his jaw would likely have cleaned the floor. He tried to stay calm and look at the couple, but now that he knew, the relationship seemed obvious.

The pair looked at each other like schoolkids with a crush. She giggled at the sound of his voice and, for a moment, looked ten years younger than before.

"Well, that's not what I would have expected for an alibi," he finally mustered.

Newman settled back on the seat and sighed. "Well, you might as well hear the whole story. I met Patsy down South during the war. She was a slave. She'd had a pretty hard life. When we heard that Lincoln had signed that emancipation order, we were just north of Atlanta. The Rebs started firing for all they was worth. I was hit. A Reb ball pretty much shattered the bone in my lower leg. I knew it would probably have to come off, but I didn't want to give myself up to the Rebs. I'd heard the stories about the prison camps—if I'd only known it was worse. I knew my leg would come off if I was captured. So I hid out in an abandoned barn. Patsy heard my moans and come to see about me. She was working at a neighboring farm, helping with the little ones. She took care of me for a few days, but the Rebs caught up with me before they left the area. I couldn't put up much of a fight and surrendered."

Grant nodded. He'd heard from one of the men in town that Newman had served under Sherman in the march to the sea. That one expedition had significantly shortened the war and saved Lincoln's reelection. Grant figured it would be a few years before Sherman's name could be spoken in the South, except when preceded by a curse word.

"Anyway," Newman continued, "after the war, we came back through that way. We'd already found the gold, Young was dead, and the rest of us weren't faring all that well. I'd had my leg amputated in Andersonville. I didn't get any ether, just sawed off at the knee. It was hard as hell to ride for any length of time, so I decided to stop off and thank the woman who took care of me. Well, I won't be too specific, but she was in a pretty bad way by the time I got there. Nothing to eat, Sherman had burnt it all. Nowhere to live, and the landowners had taken it out on her for helping a Yankee. I took one look at her again and knew that I wanted to repay her kindness."

Grant looked at the two of them. They appeared happy—even if no one knew of their true relationship. Grant had to admit that he'd never foreseen these consequences in freeing the slaves. He couldn't imagine that a presidential candidate could ever get away with this type of forbidden love, but what difference did it make to Newman, who had enough money as it was. Provided that they could find the hiding place for the gold.

He hoped the man had set some of it aside. But with that much available, why would he have bothered? Grant didn't know what Newman could do without the money. Farming required two legs and usually a family's worth of help.

"So she rode back with me. She actually made the journey a lot easier. Patsy sat behind me astride the horse and held on to me around the waist. Well, after 400 miles like that, you get to know someone. Originally, I'd just brought her back as an act of charity, but as we talked and grew close, I wanted more. I love her, Sam."

Grant was glad that Julia wasn't present. He was far more tolerant of the former slave population than she was. He saw the people in terms of humanity, troops, and politics; Julia remembered them as her playmates and the people who tended to her needs. She viewed them as kindly caretakers and semi-family. In her world, the seamier side of slavery didn't exist. The Dents didn't rend apart families or use the slaves for their own deviant pleasures.

But his father only told stories from the fanatical side of abolition. Jesse regaled his family with sordid tales of inhumanity to convince them and anyone who would listen that slavery was an abomination.

"She resisted at first, but finally she admitted that she was fond of me too. So we've been hiding this from the town ever since."

Grant stroked his beard and tried to follow the story to its conclusion. "So I don't understand how Mrs. Halley fits into all this. You could be sleeping with her as well."

Newman shook his head. "Clarissa found me and Patsy together one day. We were sharing a hug in the kitchen, and she came in the front way. Like I told you, many times we don't hear people at the front door. She saw us and became a staunch ally to us here."

Grant wondered why a small-town country woman had taken up the rallying cry for a cause that even the most fervent abolitionists didn't advocate. He'd be hard-pressed to see Charles Sumner or Harriet Beecher Stowe take a similar stance in miscegenation. "Do many people know about you two here?"

Patsy shook her head. "We can't tell folk, General. We'd be run out of town."

Newman shrugged. "She wants to keep it quiet, so we do. She stays with me, cooks and cleans, and the world thinks of us as servant and homeowner. A natural arrangement for a widower. They don't need to know anything more."

Patsy cackled. "For all the world, a wife might as well be a housecleaner. We don't get to vote or do much of nothing. I'm findings it's not a big step up from slave."

Grant knew that Julia would disagree. Despite the limitations put on his wife by society, she still stood at the helm of their family ship. She had raised the two older boys while living a continent apart from him and still took care of their needs. The two before him would not be having children, so that issue would be moot.

"Will you keep our secret?" Newman's face was the pleading look of innocent youth.

Grant knew that it would just be a matter of time before more people saw what was happening and the outrage started. For some in this part of the country, their relationship would be worse than if Mrs. Halley *had* kilt her husband. Grant had heard of Southerners who lynched men for this kind of behavior.

"I won't tell a soul, on my honor. So what do you know about Clarissa Halley and Adam Woerner?" Grant tried to steer the conversation back to the murders and away from personal distractions. He operated better on the plane of strategy than with human emotions.

"I don't know," Newman replied. "I mean, it's possible. Woerner was known for that. He charmed a few women in Belle Island. One of them tried to help him escape. That's why they shipped him to Andersonville. The Rebs didn't know how much pillow talk she'd done. They was concerned that she'd told him things that could get back to the Feds, being so close to the line and all."

Grant decided not to press his host anymore. He'd learned enough to safely rule out Newman's affair with Mrs. Halley. Still, that left the widow and the second victim of the killer. Grant stood up, and Patsy joined suit.

He went off in search of his wife and son, glad that he didn't have to hide his love from the world.

Chapter · 15

GRANT HEARD SOUNDS at the top of the stairs and decided to join his family. He was sure that Julia was anxious to learn everything which had transpired downstairs. She was not one who took kindly to being left out of things, and he rarely excluded her from anything troubling his mind. Little Jess, though, was still too young to hear the affairs of adults. The Grants tried to shield their children against life's darker side. Grant wasn't sure how well they would be able to protect their children in an environment like Washington, D.C., where fallen women practically camped on every street corner. Politics and prostitution were the two big draws in the nation's capital.

For all its isolated aspects, a town like Bethel was a good place to raise children. Grant had enjoyed his years in Ohio, even though he rarely returned to this part of the world for more than a few days at a time. At this juncture in his life, he really couldn't call anywhere home. No matter how many cities gave him houses, he was still a vagabond. There would be enough time to sit at home after his stint in the White House.

He made it to the top of the stairs and slowly opened the door to the room, in case Jess was already sleeping. After a hard day of running around and whooping, the boy sometimes couldn't keep his eyes open past dusk. The door creaked, and Grant heard a series of scuffling noises from inside. He opened the door the rest of the way to see a figure brush behind the curtains.

Grant entered the room to find it in total disarray. The trunks had been opened, carpetbags scattered on the floor. A dagger protruded from the top of one steamer trunk, an ominous beacon of the intrusion. He was glad that Julia and Jess weren't here to see the mess. They didn't need to think that there was danger around this small town.

He marched across the room and looked out the window, but the person had skedaddled, long gone into the night. A porch stretched along the second floor around to the front side of the home. The thief could easily have jumped from anywhere along here. Grant tried to look over the edge of the upper-level porch, but he couldn't tell where someone had escaped. The crisp night air invigorated his senses, but there was nothing to learn. The landscape was quiet beyond the chirp of crickets.

He went back to the room and sighed. He thought about asking Patsy to do the cleanup, but after Newman's recent admission, that might be considered crass.

Grant had managed to stuff everything back into the trunks and had started on the carpetbags when Julia and Jess entered the room.

"Land sakes, Ulys. What are you doing to our clothes?" Julia came over to inspect his work, more methodical about her packing strategies than any of Grant's generals.

"I didn't do anything. I found them this way when I came upstairs." He picked up a pair of long johns and stuffed them to the bottom of the bag. "Someone has been going through our things."

Jess gripped a rolled-up tube of paper and waved it like a

baton. "At least they didn't get the map. I've had it with me the whole time."

Grant scooped up an armful of clothes from the floor and deposited them in the last of the bags, and the room looked somewhat presentable. Whoever had been here obviously had not found what he was looking for. The destruction had been contained to their luggage. The bedding and furniture were intact and the hand-stitched quilt undisturbed. Grant knew these were no souvenir hunters come calling. The intruder had wanted the map, just as Jess claimed.

Grant looked at his wife, who possessed an annoyed air about her. She wasn't happy to have a stranger paw through her petticoats and bustles. She was a private and proper woman. If the treasure hunt had the air of a picnic before, now it would hold much higher stakes in the estimation of Julia Grant. She did not suffer intrusions gladly.

She hurried Jess off to the bathing room. Patsy had left a tub of steaming water for the boy, apparently aware of how dirty a seven year old could get. Julia left him splashing and came back to join her husband.

Grant waited while his wife did a quick inventory of their possessions. He was amazed at how fast she worked, a woman used to servants and slaves. He recalled their years at Hard-scrabble and how she had pitched in to make money for the homestead.

"Nothing is missing, Ulys. But you didn't expect that there would be, did you?" She stood up and brushed lint from the front of her navy-colored dress. The high lace collar reminded him of Mrs. Brown.

"Not really." Grant proceeded to tell her everything that had happened downstairs with Newman and Patsy. Julia pressed her lips into a thin line during several points in the story, but she never spoke a contrary word against her host.

When Grant explained how he'd seen the intruder escape, a glint came into her eyes. She looked around the room again and frowned. "The Browns. It had to be the Browns. That . . . woman and her tatting."

Grant shook his head. "Anyone could have broken in and looked for the map. I think that the whole town has to know that we were digging in an abandoned lot yesterday."

"But by all rights, the Browns—"

"By all rights, the money belongs to the United States Treasury, but I'm pretty sure that Hugh McCulloch didn't rummage through our unmentionables. Barring the Secretary, anyone in this town has just as legitimate a right to the money as Newman or Brown."

"So when you find the money, you'll be giving it back to the government?" Julia asked with a sigh.

Grant could see the way her mind worked. She was probably already imagining the headlines that the papers would print if he returned thousands of dollars in gold back to the Federal government: GRANT WON THE WAR AND THEN PAID FOR IT. He would have a reputation for honesty that would be unparalleled in American history. He watched silently as her brain tumbled over the ideas and the possibilities.

He decided to continue talking. Julia was always the helpful sounding board for his thoughts, as well as his biggest champion. During the war, she had referred to him as "Victor" and "Alexander" to laud him for the work he was doing in battle. "We really can't discount anyone in town from having invaded our room."

Julia came back to the present from the White House and looked at him. "From the sounds of it, we can eliminate your friend Mr. Newman and that Patsy. They couldn't have been in two places at once."

"Agreed. As I said before, there's no need for Newman to

steal something that he has access to at any time. But you're right. The Browns are the most likely suspects. They don't have the gold, and they're not sitting on the map. Either one of them could be concerned enough to try to take the map." Grant tried to imagine the pair scampering across the second-floor porch and jumping to safety. Neither Micah Brown nor his large wife seemed a likely candidate.

Julia stood up and went to check on Jess. She came back with a few stray water spots on her dress, which made Grant think that the boy was getting along well. "Then it could have been a woman who was here?" she offered.

He paused for a second and nodded. "I only saw a bit of shadow, not the person. Still, it wasn't a big figure, maybe five-foot-five or six, so it could have been a woman." Grant was keenly aware of his own short stature and drew himself up to his full height as he spoke.

"Then we can't exclude that dreadful Mrs. Halley," Julia huffed. "She's just as able as anyone."

No telling why the woman had received that character evaluation, but Grant knew that she must have performed some snub to earn Julia's enmity. A social misstep would be enough to hang the woman in his wife's book.

"She has every reason to steal the map," Julia went on. "She's likely to have some insight into where Woerner hid the gold because of her relationship with him, and she doesn't stand to gain anything from the current arrangement."

Grant cleared his throat, knowing his coming defense would fall on deaf ears. Julia could be adamant in her opinions. "To be fair, Julia, Mrs. Halley doesn't seem the type. She was rather offended receiving that money, and she made a point of tithing from it. It hardly seems in character for her to skulk around here, trying to steal the map. Whoever did that wants the gold and doesn't mind breaking the law to get it. That hardly sounds like a God-fearing woman like Mrs. Halley."

Julia scoffed, a skill she'd developed from years of practice as a Dent. Grant knew that she'd inherited the ability from her father, who had scoffed his way through the entire war. "Ulys, there's never been a person who wouldn't agree that it's much easier to be well-off than poor. Mrs. Halley is about to find out what that's like, and I can guarantee that she won't enjoy it. So she certainly could be after the map. Or her son, for that matter. He's a bit older than Jess, and look how much our son is into this treasure hunt."

Grant smiled, knowing that Julia had known both extremes and much preferred the good life. "But if you're going to talk about people profiting, then we should include the reverend as well. He's been making a pretty penny off the widow."

Julia tried not to smile. "You'd like that, wouldn't you? Putting the reverend away would definitely get your mother's goat. If we're going to talk about people with motives for wanting the money, you should find out who receives Mr. Woerner's estate. There's no wife or children, so someone has to get all of that. Would the gold technically belong to that person?"

Grant shrugged. "I think not. If we're going to ignore the government's rightful claim on it, the gold still would belong to the two remaining men to be spent as they see fit. The women and children would only get a portion of what they would otherwise."

"So what do we do now? Just sit here until someone succeeds in taking the map or killing someone else? Won't everything be resolved when it's down to one man? He'll be the killer. Then the whole matter will be solved." Julia stood up again and started towards the bathing room.

Grant wondered. He hated to see the men killed like this. They had suffered through so much in Andersonville that he almost felt that they deserved the compensation from a grateful

Union. Maybe not quite the sum they'd found, but an easier life seemed reasonable to him. After all, a nice new house in Philadelphia awaited Grant, not to mention the one in Galena. With a potential political career, there were rumors that some wealthy patrons were trying to find him a suitable house in Washington, too. "What if the person who tried to steal the map isn't the same one who killed Woerner and Halley? I don't think we should lynch a person just for trying to steal a map."

Julia stopped and put a hand on her hip. Apparently convicting innocent people was acceptable punishment for pawing through her clothes. "Are you suggesting that we have one person killing the men who have the gold and yet another stealing maps? It's a bit much for a small town."

"Still, the person who is responsible for killing the men here would be remiss in killing the person who doled out the gold without first knowing where it is. That's just plain tomfoolery."

Julia put a hand on the doorknob. "Why don't you just get the two of them in a room and ask them who did it? That would be the simplest thing to do."

Grant pondered the suggestion for a moment. While Julia had not been serious, he thought that perhaps an evening of reminiscences might loosen a few tongues. Of course, if he had a chance to drink and smoke, all the better. But it was all in the name of protecting the treasury and aiding the Union. Not even Julia could object to that.

CHAPTER · 16

GRANT TOOK A DRAG on his cigar and blew the smoke out slowly. Life could be good indeed. Julia had suggested a game of euchre the night before, but he'd thrown in the stogies and booze without too much fuss from his wife. Newman had offered to host the gathering, and during the day Grant had invited his father and Brown to make it a foursome. Despite his intentions of asking some difficult questions, Grant wanted to make it as much like a fun evening as possible.

Jesse, of course, had wanted to attend. He saw a chance for a quick dollar out of the men who had brought home a fortune. His eyes had lit up at the opportunity to fleece the men.

Grant was teamed up with Newman, leaving Jesse with Brown. Having Brown's wandering mind as a partner would make the pair less likely to make any money. Jesse wouldn't rig the game in his son's favor; he was never inclined to do so. But Grant knew that he'd have to keep an eye on his father, or else the old man would be plotting some crooked deal for himself and Brown.

More than one life had been lost in Grant's days in California over a bad play in the card game. He'd never played much during his days out West. There had been other schemes and plans to make money back then. Of course, the logging and potato crops had been disastrous. Games of chance might have been a better investment for his savings.

The game had been a particular favorite of Simon Bolivar Buckner, back when he and Grant were friends. The general didn't figure that Buckner would want much to do with him after Fort Donelson. The Confederate officer, when offering the fort's surrender, had hoped for better terms. Instead, Grant would not negotiate, yielding himself yet another nickname using his initials: "Unconditional Surrender Grant." Buckner had accepted the stipulation, but he was still a bit put out by the matter.

The three other men seemed at ease with the game and quickly went about the motions of throwing money on the table. Grant took his time, enjoying the cigar and the boisterous company of men who had left the women behind for the night. Unless something turned up quick, he was going to have to turn his meager evidence over to Sheriff Crosson the next day and leave it to the law to figure out what had happened. That would pretty much guarantee that they would never see the gold again. The fortune might be better off staying lost if Crosson got involved. If found, the money could lead to criminal charges and more incarceration for the two remaining men.

The veterans seemed oblivious to those facts. Newman looked a little uncomfortable, but Brown was nearly catatonic. He sat in his chair, studying his five cards as if his life depended on it. Grant had hoped that time away from Mrs. Brown might loosen his friend up, but it hadn't seemed to help much.

The foursome was almost too polite to start with. At least there wouldn't be any accusations of cheating during the game. The deck looked new, unlike the many handmade cards with their frayed and tattered corners which had been used during the war. Grant picked up his five cards and eyed the ace of clubs faceup on the small pile of cards remaining on the table. Newman, as dealer, would be expected to pick that card up if they wanted to attempt the three tricks necessary to win a hand.

Brown named clubs as trumps and threw down a dollar. Grant bit his lip but didn't speak. His friend could afford the money, even if it meant Mrs. Brown would have to make do with less lace. Grant, holding two clubs in his hand, wasn't sure how his friend planned to make the tricks.

The cards fell quickly, and Grant was amazed that Brown picked up four of the five tricks in the hand. His father smiled as he collected the coins for the partners. Jesse had won money by default, just his luck.

Newman laughed and threw down two more coins. "Just like old times, eh, Micah? You always were a lucky bastard."

Brown smiled for a second, showing a row of teeth that looked like dry field corn. The man must have been ravaged by the poor nutrition in the prison camp. He pitched a dollar bill on the table this time. "Weren't so lucky that I didn't end up in Andersonville, eh?"

Newman shrugged. "True enough, but you always ended the game with the most sticks by far."

"Sticks don't get you much in a prison camp, Zeke. You should know that. Didn't help those men one bit." For a moment, Grant thought that Brown was going to bawl.

The general had seen men come out of Andersonville broken, but he hadn't known them before the war. It was just the way it was. This was like seeing a friend's children all grown up. You couldn't believe the change in them after the passage of time. For the people you knew best, you didn't see the slow changes in appearance. He knew that Majors Rawlins and Badeau had aged because of the war, but it didn't register with him because he had shared four years with them. He had always been amazed at how much Lincoln had aged each time he'd come to camp, but it was nothing like his friends. Grant had worried that his own potential presidency would age him too quickly, but it was easier still than the prison camps.

Jesse got ready for the next hand. The men bet again, falling into a routine of Grant and his father going first, followed by Newman and Brown. Jesse seemed to enjoy his role as dealer and snatched up the jack of diamonds when the bid came around to him. Grant wasn't sure why Newman and Brown didn't fare better with the cards. After all, by their own admission, they'd spent many a day wiling away the hours at euchre. Brown had trouble keeping the cards straight, often forgetting that same-suit jacks trumped the ace. He would throw down a card, only to have to pull it back up and throw another. On more than one occasion, he had to put a card back in his hand.

Newman opted to go first and placed a dollar on the table. Brown took the man's lead and placed a greenback as his bet. Grant put down a single coin again, knowing that these men had much more money to waste on pastimes.

Jesse threw his cards out slowly. Even with the bower, which all the men at the table pronounced "barr," he and Brown were euchred, and forked over the money to Grant and Newman. Grant scooped up a few coins for his trouble. Not that it made a huge difference, but perhaps Julia would like a new dress for her upcoming Cincinnati social events. He planned the way to explain to her the source of all the money, since the game had been set up with the specific purpose of trying to learn more from the men about what was going on—not come back with a pocketful of cash.

The night wore on with Grant slowly bringing up his totals until he felt sure enough to bet with the greenbacks that Jesse seemed to hand to him on a more regular basis. He pocketed some of the money, enjoying for a few minutes the illusion of wealth. He'd never had much of it, forced to make do and ask for handouts from his father, who doled out money like a miser.

Newman grew more verbal as the bottles were slowly drained. Brown actually got some color in his face and seemed to enjoy life for a few minutes. He laughed out loud for the first time since Grant had been in town. This was more like the old kicker that Grant had known when he was visiting from West Point.

Brown emptied another glass of bourbon and looked at Newman. "I miss Young, you know?" He wiped his mouth off with the back of his hand.

"Yup, I miss them both," Newman replied. "Doesn't seem right here without them."

"Well, maybe not Woerner. I got a mite tired of him whining abouts every little thing. But yeah, I miss Halley too." Brown took another sip from his glass that Grant had filled when no one was looking. The man didn't seem to notice that his glass never emptied. "You know that Providence Springs was in the deadline? Have you ever been to Island Number Ten?"

Grant winced to think of Andersonville's lack of facilities. Brown was referencing the natural spring that fell just outside the perimeter of the camp. Men who tried to reach the spring were shot on sight. Like those Greek myths, nourishment was plainly visible, but never to be reached.

Newman shook his head. "Nah, Micah. They've never been there. Just you and me."

Brown seemed to accept the answer and went back to studying his cards.

"Why not Woerner?" Jesse looked at the men with wide eyes. He hadn't been drinking. Maybe he thought that his wife would be able to see the accumulations of her God's sins if they came all in one night. Grant could hardly imagine what Hannah would say if she saw Jesse dealing cards for euchre. Her strict Methodist background would have prevented any such gambling, especially the type that went on in a saloon hall.

Brown sniffed and looked around like he couldn't believe someone was talking to him. "He got himself some big-city ways. We was all from the same village, but he spent some time in Atlanta before he got sent to camp. Of course, the town was deserted, but he never forgot all the things he saw there. Made him want more."

Grant nodded. He'd seen many men who would never go back to farming a small Indiana or Illinois homestead after experiencing the rest of the country. The wide Atlantic Ocean, the mighty Mississippi, the Appalachian Mountains in fall. Going back to plow the same fields for the rest of their lives had no appeal after seeing the majesty of the United States

Brown pointed a crooked finger at Grant, so that it seemed to point to the table. "Woerner wanted to take all that gold home and parcel it out."

"Why did you let him?" Grant still wondered why they had all allowed one of their group to keep the gold. The result meant that none of them would receive another cent at this point.

"Woerner thought the whole thing out," Newman said. "He was afraid that someone would figure out what had happened and try to make off with the money."

Brown spat in the cuspidor by the table. "He was the only one what would make off with the money. He wanted to bring it home."

Newman smiled and patted Brown's shoulder. "That's not entirely true. I remember Halley picking up a handful of coins and trying to stuff them in his pockets and nearly falling down from all the extra weight on him. Admit it, we all wanted the money. Hell, we deserved it."

Brown flipped a gold coin to Grant. "It's not like the money belonged to anyone. It was just sitting there."

Grant raised an eyebrow. "It was the gold of the Confederate government. By all rights that belongs to the Federals. The spoils of war go the victor and all that."

Brown played with another coin. The gold glinted as it wended between his fingers. "I'm a Federal and a victor too, Sam. And after what I'd been through, a little money for my troubles only seemed fair."

"We weren't supposed to profit from the war. What about all those boys who lost their lives?" Grant felt his face flush. These men had forgotten what the war was to be fought over. Not money, but to preserve an idea and to make men free. Certainly Newman—with his interest in an ex-slave woman—should realize that.

"They won't be needing it now, will they?" Brown's eyes were as hard as iron as he looked at the pot on the table.

"That's no way to talk. Those boys gave their all for the Union, so there would be a single nation."

Brown snorted and stopped playing with the coin. He slid it back into his pocket and put his hand on the table. "C'mon, Sam. Be real. It weren't like you didn't profit from the war. You started out a failure. No offense, but you didn't amount to much out of a uniform. And now look at you. You're a big man now, and I know those people in Philadelphia bought you a house. A house. And how much money did New York give you? So don't tell me that you didn't profit from the war. And if you did, there's no reason I shouldn't either."

"But I didn't take anything that wasn't given to me. That gold is something different."

"How many times did we take things from the Rebs when we finished a battle? Supplies, food, horses. Hell, Sherman ate his way through Georgia. So if I come across some gold coins, who's to say that I shouldn't take what I want?"

"But scavenging for food is a necessity. Money is not." Grant knew that he'd been considered a maverick for cutting his own supply lines and making his troops scour the countryside for something to eat. The military scholars at West Point would have had a conniption to think of such a tactic. But he'd kept the looting to a minimum even as the men searched for something to eat.

"I look at them as reparations," Brown said. "You replaced food when you were hungry. You replaced a horse if yours got shot. They took away more than my food at Andersonville. They took away my dignity. I saw things in that place that no man should see. I can't even begin to tell you what Newman and me had to stand. Weren't right. No man should have to deal with that." The memories seemed to wrack his body. He turned his face away for a moment.

Grant downed his drink and looked for the bottle. He wasn't good with the emotions and pains of his former troops. He remembered the agonized cries of the boys in the wilderness, boys who would not return home. They'd been burned alive by the brush fires set by the constant gunfire. He hadn't thrown thousands of boys into battle for a profit. He'd done it to save the Union—to preserve a single nation. Why didn't people see that? If people wanted to thank him, he couldn't stop them, but he hadn't done any of it for the glory or the fame, or especially the money. "I just don't think it's right."

Brown looked down at the coins on the table. He had lost money playing euchre, but it didn't seem to bother him at all. "Why don't you ask your father about that? I heard he made a pretty penny during the war."

"There was a need for leather," Jesse said.

"And of course he was there to fill that need." Brown rolled his eyes and carried on as though Jesse was not in the state, much less the same room. "I heard he made a great deal of money from the government. I'm sure that had nothing to do with you, Sam."

The man Grant had known from his summers in Bethel was gone, replaced by an older, more skeptical soul. Grant wasn't sure how to react. His friend was right, of course. Jesse had made a fortune during the war; by his own account, he'd earned over $100,000. A veritable Midas touch in leather.

Jesse merely smiled and raked in the coins from the last turn. He didn't seem to mind the accusations, wearing them almost as a badge of honor.

Grant decided that the evening had come to an end. He took one last drink of whiskey before pulling back from the table. The other men took his lead one last time and collected the smaller sums that they brought away from the table. Jesse counted out the money from the last hand. The rest he tucked safely into his vest. He patted Grant on the shoulder and gave him a slight push in the right direction.

Fortunately, Grant had only to navigate the stairs to get to bed. He tried to be silent as he opened the door, only to find Julia still awake and waiting for him.

CHAPTER · 17

GRANT SMILED as he saw the warm family scene, even though he knew that he would catch the devil from his wife for drinking and smoking. A fire lapped the logs in the hearth. Julia read a book, something she'd picked up downstairs in Newman's library. She had her back to the door, but she turned to face her husband as he entered.

Little Jess was on the bed, still puzzling over the map like a cipher. Grant had suspected before going downstairs that Julia didn't have the resolve to get their son into bed while Grant was out trying to gather clues to the boy's riddle. A shame that the lad didn't apply himself to schoolwork with the same vim.

The map was spread out over the comforter like a giant jigsaw puzzle, and Jess pored over the lines and streets like so many pieces to solve. Looking up as Grant entered the room, he leapt up as though he hadn't seen him in years, rather than just hours before. He greeted his father with a big hug and quickly found the coins in his pocket. Grant immediately knew he'd been overreached in the show of affection.

"Look at all these." Jess took a stack of them and neatly made a single column. He held them in one hand and feigned an expression of awe. "Now I'm just like Grandfather."

Jess had developed a sense of mimicry well beyond his years. The story of his imitation of his father's speeches—standing up, hemming and hawing for a few seconds, muttering a few words followed by a quick exit—was legendary. He'd done it in such a way that accentuated Grant's awkwardness at public address.

Now again, the lad had shown a sharp insight into his grandfather's personality. Jesse Root Grant's mannerisms were captured in miniature in Jess. Julia laughed with more exuberance than the performance warranted. Grant knew that she felt her father-in-law to be a common man who worshipped at the altar of the almighty dollar, but she neglected to see that her own father kept up a façade of wealth long past the time when his wallet could afford it.

Grant snatched the coins from the boy's hand and threw them onto the bed. Jess threw a glance to the coins as they landed on the bed, but he stayed focused on his father. No telling if the little dodger had found the greenbacks too.

Julia smiled at her husband. "Well, it looks like you did well for yourself. Hopefully you were able to do as well in finding out more about what is going on in town."

Grant decided to show off a bit. The booze had loosened him up enough to want to display his prowess at making money, something that he'd never accomplished before the war. He took the stack of greenbacks and threw them onto the dresser. They slid over and landed on the lace doily that Mrs. Brown had tatted.

Jess let out a whoop that would wake anyone who'd been trying to sleep. Fortunately, that would be only Patsy; Grant was sure that Newman couldn't have made it into bed quite yet.

Jess picked up the lace napkin and the bills from the dresser and threw them with another shout onto the bed. The greenbacks fluttered down to the covers like a viridian snow.

The doily landed on the map. For a moment, Grant didn't

speak. Julia's lecture to her son about the noise, and Jess's protestations of innocence, didn't register in his ears. He could only look at the map, the lace, and the bedspread. Suddenly, he knew what Woerner had done and why he'd had the doily made special. His scheme was worthy of anything that rogue Mosby had ever dreamed up.

He quickly moved over to the bed and brushed the dollars out of the way. If he was right, there would be more money to be had than what was on the bed right now. He began to subtly shift the lace over the map, trying to locate the X marks through the odd pattern of tatting. He found one corner that seemed to match an X on the map and started trying to line up a second marker. Bethel's perpendicular streets made for an easy time. Math had been one of his strong suits at West Point, and given the way this grid was set up, matching two points from the map to the lace should align the rest of the marks to the lace.

This had been what Woerner had meant when he marked the Bible passage. The servant had hidden the coins in a napkin, and so had he. The napkin was a filter that changed an ordinary street map into a treasure map. Grant knew that he was on the right track. This convoluted thought process was the way the dead man's mind had operated when Grant had known him. Nothing was as it seemed. Apart, the two items were useless. It was only when added together that the meaning became clear.

As Grant struggled to find the two matching points, he shifted the linen again and then inched it towards West Street. Of course, Woerner hadn't done it so that the corners matched up. That might have been too simple. The napkin was smaller, and as Grant moved the linen, it was at an odd angle to the sides of the map.

Finally, he found the two points and pressed the sides down

so that the two were practically joined. The X that had marked the center of the napkin pointed to a location on Charity Street. That was Woerner's twisted sense of humor coming back again. With a certain nostalgia induced by Kentucky grain, Grant remembered the way Woerner would play word games with his friends. He snapped out of it and creased the map under the X so that they could look there in the morning.

Jess could barely contain himself. He kept poking at the spot on the map that Grant had identified. The boy had already suggested twice that they start digging now, but Grant was in no shape for the exertion. Besides, the September nights got cool, and he didn't fancy finding the gold while contracting a head cold. He finally got his son into bed, though he wasn't sure if the boy would sleep.

Julia put down her book and approached the bed. Grant noticed that she'd been reading one of the little penny dreadfuls. Newman's house seemed chock-full of them. She must have been bored to resort to such reading. Julia prided herself on improving her mind. She looked at the map and where Grant had marked the location. "Ulys, did you keep the key?"

He shook his head. "No. As far as I know, Newman still has it."

She took a deep breath and sighed, a soft breeze against his neck. "Then we'll have to tell him about it, won't we?"

Grant smiled. This attitude was coming from a woman who couldn't understand why the men wouldn't have shipped the money directly to the government. Now she wanted to hoard it for herself. Gold fever infected everyone to some degree. "I would have told him anyway."

Julia pressed her lips into a thin line. "Maybe we don't need the key to get the gold. We could go look."

He knew that the key was a part of the solution to Woerner's puzzle. He wasn't sure how it could fit in or even if the gold would be there. For all Grant knew, the location could merely be another indicator in a series of pointers that led to the gold.

Woerner had thought that he should have gone to West Point instead of Grant, destined for greater things. At the time, the only thing Grant had wanted from the academy was a career as a mathematics teacher. Little had he known what the future held.

Most likely, the key unlocked a vault or some kind of bank box that held the coins. He didn't know how the Confederates had stored their gold when they left Richmond. That had been a harried time. Men had been stuffed into railroad boxcars, trying to escape from the impending attack of the city.

The government had fled to Danville, taking as much as they could with them. But Grant didn't know how the gold had been transported. It was heavy, so presumably they had carried the fortune in containers. The primary focus had been to keep the provisions and goods out of the hands of the Federals. All else in those days had been secondary.

The Cabinet and the other government figures were justly worried that they would be charged with treason and executed. It made them react in ways that Grant couldn't imagine. That irrational fear made them scatter across the country as the inevitability of defeat came upon them. Members of the Cabinet took small boats to Cuba to escape punishment. Realistically, all the Federal government asked of the Confederate leadership was that they had not materially profited from the war. Ironic, considering that he was now looking for the remains of their treasury.

By turn, Washington hadn't felt the hot breath of the Rebs on its home turf. Even the proximity of Washington and Richmond had not made the Senate quiver with fear of destruction. Despite the forays into the Washington area by General Early at the end of the war, Sheridan had never let the attacks get out of hand. Grant had never seriously considered an enemy invasion of Washington to be possible while he was at the helm of the Army of Virginia.

Despite the sacrifices that Newman had made for the Federals, for some reason Julia still didn't approve of passing along the information about the map. Grant hoped it wasn't because of whom the man chose to court. Julia could be quite arbitrary in her dislikes. He had seen that in the past.

"I just wish you wouldn't tell anyone until after we find the money," she said. "For all we know, we could be inviting a murderer to tag along."

Grant thought about it but didn't see Newman as the killer. He couldn't put his finger on the reason why, but as sure as he'd won the night's euchre game, he knew that Newman hadn't killed those men. Besides, Newman and Patsy were the only two who couldn't have gone after the map. They'd been downstairs with him, and Newman's infirmity made it impossible for him to jump off the balcony to the ground below.

So Newman was about the only person Grant felt safe in ruling out from the shenanigans in town. Everyone else he knew could be responsible for the murders of multiple men and for the burglary of their room. Plus he wouldn't trust Julia or Jess with a gun, and he wanted someone to watch his back the next day when he went looking for the gold.

Chapter · 18

THE NEXT MORNING broke crisp and clean, the type of morning where the frosted grass crackles under the feet like eggshells. Jess had insisted on an early start, more because he couldn't sleep than anything else. In the shared sleeping quarters, that meant that neither Grant nor Julia slept either.

Newman and Patsy stumbled to the kitchen, hearing all the ruckus. Newman had pulled on a shirt, but no pants, which served to call attention to the gaping hole where his leg should have jutted from the shirttails.

Grant tried not to gawk at the jagged red stump that occasionally peeked through. He tried not to speculate if the couple had come from the same room in the back of the house. He felt that some level of decorum and privacy should be maintained, especially among public figures. He would no more enjoy someone openly discussing his personal life.

Jess had accumulated several pieces of digging equipment in the middle of the floor. Enough shovels, pickaxes, and spades to tunnel to Cincinnati if need be. Grant envied the enthusiasm of youth, where a young man didn't think of the moral ramifications of money.

The boy didn't care if the money had been used to kill Federal soldiers or to hold on to a lifestyle that held blacks as subhuman. To him, a treasure existed and needed to be found. All other concerns rested far from the center of attention. For the same reasons, Grant had purposely not invited his father, not knowing what schemes Jesse would develop to handle the money.

After Grant explained the entire story of the map and the lace napkin, Patsy started making coffee for the group. She methodically went about her business, as if locating the Confederate gold was a typical hunting trip or fishing expedition. Soon the aroma of coffee filled the kitchen. Jess squirmed in his seat, while Grant took his time to savor the aroma. He hadn't been gone from the army life so long that he couldn't remember all the bitter brews made in camp. Jess practically dragged his father towards the door.

While Grant enjoyed the coffee, Newman dressed. He came back into the kitchen with a clean pair of dress pants, the left leg pinned shut at the knee. Julia had donned a simple dress and pulled her hair back in a severe but effective bun. She didn't want to be left out of the hunt. She'd made that clear the previous night.

Patsy didn't look particularly enthused, busying herself with the dishes, while Jess and Newman compared notes on the best digging tool and what was at the site marked on the map. Jesse's tannery had been just up the street. He'd bought into the Collins tannery and run it until 1856, when he'd moved to Covington. Grant hadn't been back by there since.

Newman grabbed the pickax and carried it under his arm. Leading the way to the site on Charity, he seemed to manage with the utensil and his crutches. Grant followed, quiet in his own thoughts as Jess jabbered on about treasures and pirates. Julia walked beside her husband and slid her arm through his as if the excursion was nothing more than a brisk morning stroll.

Of course, Grant rarely carried spades when walking with his wife, but that was beside the point. Some pretense could exist this morning.

The location was another empty lot. The land had once held a house, but the charred foundation indicated that the structure had burnt down some time ago. Only a few bricks from the hearth and pieces of wood remained. No chimney, no glass, and no discarded or melted possessions. Grant couldn't discern anything about the one-time occupants. Either they had been able to remove their possessions before the fire, or the destruction had been complete. The tall grasses that would have covered the remains in summer had begun to wilt, exposing the blackened masonry.

Grant threw down his shovel at the edge of the road and began to look for the marker. He assumed that Woerner had at least pinpointed the location of the gold. Even he wouldn't make it so difficult that any seeker would have to dig up an entire lot. "When did this house burn down?"

Newman shrugged. "Five, six years ago. Before I went off to war, for sure. Why?"

Grant kicked at the grass. No sign of a marker at all. The fire had taken place long before Woerner had come home with the gold, so that meant the marker had not been destroyed by the blaze. Things were just as they would have been when he returned in May. Still, Grant couldn't see how the key helped them. From his vantage point, there were no doors left standing in the old house, so no locks for a key.

The troop wandered the plot aimlessly, trying to find a sign of where the gold could be. Another clue perhaps. Or a sign to point the direction. Grant was making circles, coming closer and closer to the burnt-out house. He stopped suddenly and started tracing the foundation of the building. He made steps in a clockwise fashion, walking at first and then beginning to trot. He stopped abruptly and motioned for the others to join him.

The old root cellar stood on the far side from Charity Street. Unless you were a head taller than Grant, no one would see you standing back here from the street. Little Woerner could have come by anytime and not have been spotted. The charred remains of the home and the grasses that sloped up to the house made excellent cover. This hiding place had been given a great deal of thought.

The cellar door wasn't fastened in any manner. That surprised Grant, given what he suspected was hidden inside. He opened the door and looked into the cellar. The small wooden stairs had footprints in the dust. Grant had a feeling that he'd come to the journey's end.

He cautiously made his way down the stairs. No more than five feet in front of him was a large, solid door, fastened shut with a lock. Grant motioned for Newman, who hobbled down to join him. He put the key in the lock and easily turned it. The sweet sound of the click echoed in the cellar. Grant removed the lock and pushed the door into the room.

He'd never seen so much gold in one place. He'd seen nuggets and bars when he was in California. Men had gone crazy for a few pieces of panned gold. Men with enough gold to smelt it into a bar guarded it with their lives. And here was more gold than any fifty prospectors could have dreamt. The coins lay on the floor, spilling out of saddlebags that were slowly molding from the humid peat around them.

He didn't speak for a minute, trying to imagine what his four friends had felt, burying their comrade and finding a storehouse of Reb money for the taking. Money from the same men who had made animals of them in a prison camp. A reward for being beaten and starved and left to die from dysentery and infections. Circumstances so dire that the officers at the camp were on trial for war crimes. The amount here was barely over two dollars for each life lost in that Georgia hole.

Grant knew that, even in the best of circumstances, men would want the money. Lust after it, covet it. He'd done his best to make sure that his soldiers didn't loot when they attacked a town. Not only was it a further reason for the enemy to fight, it distracted the men from their purpose—to preserve the Union and wage a good battle. A man couldn't serve two masters, and greed was a demanding one.

Jess galloped between Grant and Newman and ran into the room. He scooped up a handful of coins and threw them into the air. The clack and tinkle of metal on metal reverberated through the little chamber. The excitement was so palatable that Grant felt as if the whole of Bethel must now know they'd found the gold. The entire village would wait for them at the top of the stairs, wanting a share.

Jess stuck his hand deep inside one of the saddlebags and left it there. The boy seemed fascinated by the sheer volume of coins in front of him. How like his namesake, Grant thought.

Grant picked up a saddlebag and was amazed at the weight. How could those broken men have managed to take all this gold with them? He wondered how much they'd left. Was the rest of the treasury still in Georgia, or had some other lucky soul found it? No telling where the entire Confederate treasury had got off to. Some had been paid out to the ragtag troops left guarding the last of the Rebel Cabinet and Davis. No one would guard gold without wanting some for himself. How much had the Confederate Cabinet absconded with? Rumors abounded regarding Butler's lifestyle out of the country. Who knew what else was tucked away, hidden in banks and overseas accounts. Grant felt sure that someday the rest of it would be recovered.

Newman took a step towards him. "What are you doing

with all that, Sam? You can't just walk out of here with it. The whole town will see you."

Grant shook his head. "This doesn't belong to you. It's already killed two men in this town, and who knows who would be next? I can't have that on my head." Crosson would be back in town shortly, and Grant would try his best to keep the men's names out of the story he'd weave for the sheriff.

Newman looked down at the saddlebag. "That's Halley's bag you're holding. Don't suppose I could just keep my bag. After all, it does belong to me."

Grant looked up from the bag and saw Julia descending the stairs. He was puzzled for a moment, trying to figure out why she would enter the cellar. This was not the type of place she cared to visit, especially when it didn't involve a chore. She was more the fresh-air-and-sunshine type of woman. Her horsemanship was nearly equal to his.

She touched her feet to the dirt floor and scurried over to her husband. He put an arm around her, feeling her shiver. He couldn't figure out what had brought out this reaction in her until he looked up again.

Mrs. Brown stood in the doorway to the cellar, carrying a rifle. "Took you folk long enough to find it. I'd begun to give up hope of getting any more money."

Newman took a step towards her. She cocked the gun and leveled it at the man. "I wouldn't be doing that, Zeke. I can use this thing if I have to."

Grant tried to combine this perception of the woman with the tatting housewife he'd met a few days earlier. Is this what gold fever did to someone? Make an ordinary person into a killer? He could see Julia slay someone to save her family or herself, but never for money. Maybe because she'd grown up with it. She'd always taken wealth as a given, but she worked without complaints when it wasn't there. In their lean years, she'd kept house and made do with what they had. She was not the type to seek out money at all costs.

Mrs. Brown took a step towards them and motioned with her gun for the group to head towards the back room of the cellar. Grant knew that she would have to kill them in order to make off with the money. She couldn't hold them hostage and take all the gold without being suspected of something. The people in the cellar would have to die in order for the treasure to be safe with her. No one else in Bethel could know, or else the government and every greedy soul in town would want it. Grant didn't know how she would be able to explain the cash to her husband, but maybe he was too far gone to care. Was he content not knowing, or was he complicit in this killing spree?

She backed them up a few more paces. Julia shielded Jess behind her skirts, one of the few times when the boy didn't protest his mother's protective nature. Newman and Grant stood in front of her, making a pyramid of sorts. Grant would have dove for Mrs. Brown would he not have jeopardized the life of his dear wife. Life without Julia would not be worth a red cent, much less a gold coin.

"You mean to kill us, Harriet?" Newman was fairly adept at moving backwards on his sticks. He retreated farther into the cellar with the rest of them. His one stick hit the doorway on the way back and nearly flew out from under his arm. He gripped it more tightly and adjusted himself. Grant could see white knuckles bear down on the wood.

"Not if I don't have to," she said as she waved the gun at the group again. She managed to lean down and retrieve the first saddlebag on the floor without moving her gun. She pitched it over her shoulder with an effort. The rifle seemed to sag a bit under the weight of the gold.

"But you killed all those other people." Grant looked for a weapon to subdue the woman, but nothing seemed close at hand. Enough money to buy bodyguards and metal-covered carriages, but none of it did any good to them now. "Why did you kill them?"

Mrs. Brown shook her head as much as she could with bags of gold hanging from her shoulders. "I didn't kill nobody. What are you talking about?"

"You killed those men for the gold, and now you mean to kill us." Grant wanted to keep her talking, giving them a few minutes of time. If he could figure out a way to save Julia and Jess, he'd do it, even if it meant the loss of his own life. He'd been in worse scrapes before, but not when his family was in peril.

Motioning with the barrel of the rifle, Mrs. Brown indicated the bag that rested to Grant's left. "Pick up that bag and hand it to me."

Newman started to take a step towards her. "When did you get so greedy? That's not yours. Why don't you take only your share?"

Her face turned up in a twisted grin. "There's only two of you left now. That means Micah gets half. He might be daft now, but I ain't." She pointed to the bags once more.

Newman stepped forward again. "But no one gets a full share until there's only one person left. There are still two. So no one gets it yet."

She pointed the gun directly at Newman. "Don't take another step, Zeke. I'm a-warning you. Don't make me use this." She turned her head to face Grant. "Now pick that bag up and hand it to me real slow like."

Grant slid his hand under the soft leather of the bag and started to heft it. Surprised at the weight, he set it back down to adjust his grip. He was trying to use just one hand, but he gave up and twisted around so that he could use both hands. He felt the bag rise easily, but he made a grunting sound as if he might be having trouble.

He hoped Mrs. Brown believed his performance. He wasn't the best of actors. She staggered under the weight of her bag; perhaps she would believe that the others weighed even more. He wasn't sure how she could lug out all of the booty without multiple trips. That left the four people unguarded. It seemed their best chance to escape.

He made another attempt to lift the bag. He swung around with all his force, hoping to strike Mrs. Brown and knock her off-balance. Instead, he felt the bag hit Newman square in the good leg. Grant watched as his plot misfired in slow motion, like a Union-issued musket.

Newman started to tumble and grabbed the hem of Grant's jacket as he fell. He forgot the crutches as he went down, and one stick flew in the air. Newman hit the ground with a thud that seemed to knock the breath out of him. The crutch caught Mrs. Brown on the arm, and the rifle jerked up in the air.

She must have pulled the trigger, because a shot went off. The sound shook the tiny cellar, and a storm of dirt fell from the ceiling where the bullet had hit. Julia and Jess hid their heads from the dirt pellets, but Mrs. Brown looked up to see where her shot had gone and received a faceful of dirt for her trouble. She sputtered and tried to wipe her eyes.

The rifle flailed wildly as she did. Grant snatched the gun by the barrel and yanked. She fell to the ground, landing almost side by side with Newman.

She didn't move as Grant pointed the gun in her direction. She must have hit her head, but he could see her still breathing, her chest moving rhythmically. He handed the gun to Newman, who now sat on the dirt floor. Newman kept his eye on the woman as Grant hefted her over his shoulder.

The general placed her gently on the floor of the back room, then came out, locking her inside with the key they'd found at Woerner's. The three other members of the treasure hunt were all standing and looking at Grant with concern. He guessed he looked a fright with clay and mud mixed in his hair and beard.

He wiped some of the dirt from his uniform and helped Julia and Jess back up the stairs. "Looks like we won't have to worry about that anymore. I'll go talk to Father about seeing what the sheriff can do regarding Mrs. Brown."

CHAPTER · 19

JESSE CAME INTO NEWMAN'S HOUSE and plopped down on the curved-back love seat. "She still is denying that she had anything to do with the murders. She said she hadn't been in Woerner's house for ages and she hadn't seen Halley for several days. Micah will back her up on that."

Grant put a hand to his head. He felt a headache coming on from the stress and the exertion of carrying all the gold back to the Newman place. They had secured it in a safe in Newman's upper floor, where it would be protected from anyone else with a hankering for gold.

Grant hadn't made contact with anyone in the Treasury Department. He wasn't sure how to broach the subject without putting his friends at risk for prosecution. They'd already done time in Andersonville for their country. He wasn't sure that he could be responsible for incarcerating them a second time. A one-legged man and a veteran who slipped back into the past wouldn't fare well in federal prison. More likely than not, they would never see freedom again, dying behind bars.

Still, he wasn't sure that he could let them keep the money in good conscience. It didn't belong to them, and the government could sorely use it to pay for a war they had financed.

Death on credit, nothing better. And to make it worse, Grant couldn't see giving any of the gold to Brown when his wife sat behind bars for the murders of two men who had protected the Union.

He hadn't talked to Newman specifically, but he knew they would have to sit down and hash matters out at some point. The two would at least need to come up with a common story for the government. The whole plan would be somewhat risky, as they couldn't predict how Mrs. Brown would act. It made the planning all that much more difficult. Still, Grant had dealt with tougher enemies in the past and won.

He looked at his father and tried to remember what he wanted to ask him. Jesse had just returned from the mayor's house. As an ex-village official, he felt that he had some rank in learning what the town planned to do with Mrs. Brown. No one in Bethel was familiar with the procedures of dealing with murderers—and a woman to boot. Murder cases were rare in Clermont County, and cold-blooded killers were unheard of. Grant remembered the fuss over hanging Mary Surratt, a coconspirator in the Lincoln assassination. The death of two veterans wouldn't compare to the death of the leader of the Union. So execution would most likely not be an option.

"She's still denying that she killed anybody. She wanted the money sure enough, but nothing more. She was firm on that." Jesse removed his glasses and polished each lens with deliberation. "I'm inclined to believe her, Ulysses. She didn't know anything about how Woerner tripped. You could see it in her face. If she don't know how he was killed, how could she have done those deeds?"

Grant flashed back to the scene in the cellar. "You didn't see her yesterday. She would have killed us all for that gold. I could see it."

"That may be, but it doesn't mean that she killed those other two men. Heck, no telling who might have killed for that money." Jesse replaced his glasses. Grant could see the thought of money and riches rush through his mind.

"So now you're suggesting that Newman or Brown killed their friends for a few dollars more? They were friends, for goodness' sake. They went through hell together. You saw them at the euchre game. How much money is enough? None of them could have spent all that money in their lifetime. What do they need with more?"

Jesse barked out a laugh. "Don't you know by now that men will never have enough money? It's just the way things are."

Grant sighed. He didn't understand men and their money. When he wanted something, he went for it and was happy to pay the price. The constant need for more didn't infect his soul. He could be content with a house that he'd built with his own hands. "So what happens now? What will be done with that woman?"

"The visiting magistrate is in town in two days. They'll bind her over for trial at that point. They let her go home. Someone needs to take care of Micah, and he doesn't have any other family in town."

Grant took a hard swallow. "I'm not sure that's a good idea. It's not like she took a gun to Woerner. She used nails and a piece of string. She's a very resourceful woman. No telling what mischief she could get into." He worried that she would arrive in no time, looking for the gold again. She'd shown that she wasn't above killing to get her hands on it. His opinion of the local constabulary had diminished significantly over the past few hours. Perhaps he would have been better served to take the matter into his own hands, as he had done so many times in war.

Jesse waved a hand, as if women could not conceivably be killers. Grant knew better. The father still felt he knew more than the son after all these years. Grant was supposed to defer to the man, even when he knew that Jesse had not seen what women were capable of during the war.

Women had killed with the same passions as men. Man or woman, it didn't mean that a person couldn't have the passions to kill. Caring, wanting, and needing crossed all boundaries. The fairer sex only seemed to get away with more, since the most chivalrous of men couldn't believe that a woman would slit a throat or shoot in cold blood.

"How is Micah taking all this? Does he understand what's happening?" Grant knew that the man hadn't seemed right when they talked. Could he comprehend that his wife had killed his friends for cash? Maybe that kind of knowledge was better off not known.

Jesse shook his head. "Who can tell with him? I can't make heads or tails of what he says or means. I don't think he'd know if he got any money or lived in a field. He's pretty far gone that way."

Grant nodded. He found it difficult enough to discern the true feelings of a man who spoke in complete sentences. Brown was an enigma to him.

Newman stepped into the room, and his gaze bounced between Grant and Jesse. He didn't speak, but sat down slowly in the chair across from the love seat. Next to him, he rested his sticks, the same pair that had so effectively taken out Mrs. Brown. "Howdy, Sam. Mr. Grant. I heard they let Harriet Brown go home."

Grant nodded and turned away from the man. His friend, the person who helped save his family, and Grant didn't know what to tell him about the gold. "You know that she won't be getting a share of the gold. The incident in the cellar should be the end of any claim the Browns have on it."

Newman looked off in the distance, out the covered windows to Main Street. "I'm sure no one will be. It will be going back to the government."

Jesse looked at his son and at their host. "Well, actually, you know, Ulysses, no one is certain who the money should go to. I mean, you assume that the gold came from the Confederate treasury, but you don't know that for a fact. It could have been someone's private store of gold or who knows what. Heck, you can't even be sure that it's from the South. Coins are coins. You'll get no tales from a piece of metal."

Grant recognized his father's stubborn streak coming out. The man could debate any subject for hours. It had made him a nuisance at the Georgetown watering holes when he'd spouted his Whig and Know-Nothing views for the world to hear. He'd angered Senator Hamer sufficiently that the two men didn't talk to each other for years. Grant had considered the congressman to be fortunate. They hadn't resumed their friendship until Jesse wanted the West Point appointment for his son.

Newman gave the men a small smile. "Well, that's true. The cargo wasn't marked to the owner. It could have been anyone's gold."

Grant rolled his eyes. "The Confederate government was leaving town in a hurry. They didn't know when or if they would be back. Of course they didn't stop to mark the cargo."

Jesse sat up straight on the love seat. "Well, without proper identification, I believe that found items belong to the person who discovers them. Isn't that the way of the world?" He tugged at his coat. Jesse made a point to look proper at all times, and he never failed to mention his son's sloppy appearance. On the other hand, Grant's sartorial role model was Zachary Taylor—Old Rough and Ready—who had also ridden military victory to the presidency. That man was interested more in winning wars rather than appearances.

Newman shrugged and gave Grant a weak grin. "I believe so."

Grant looked from one man to the other. He knew when he'd been beat. "Okay, I won't contact the Treasury, but it will have to be on a few conditions."

Newman nearly sprang to his foot. His growing smile nearly split his cheeks open. "Thank you, Sam. Thank you so much."

Jesse merely smiled at his son as he stared down his glasses at him. He didn't bother to speak.

"First," Grant began, "you can't have had anything to do with the killings. Neither you or Patsy. If you do, the money goes back to the government immediately." He crossed his arms and let it be known that he meant business. In times of battle his word was good, and he wanted the same to be felt in peacetime.

Newman looked him in the eyes and said without blinking, "I swear on my life that I had nothing to do with those deaths, Sam. Honest."

Grant longed to believe the man. He didn't want one of the last few of his Bethel friends to be a murderer. Still, he wasn't convinced that Mrs. Brown had done the killings. She'd been honest in everything else, and she continued to deny any involvement in the killings. It shook his conviction in her guilt. Why lie about that now? What did it benefit her?

He continued with his second condition. "Next, you'll need to provide something for the widows and for Brown. That kind of money should have some responsibility that goes with it."

Newman sat up a bit straighter in his seat. "Of course I would. You didn't need to tell me that. I would have done that anyways."

Grant nodded. "I figured as much, but I want there to be some clear rules for keeping the gold."

Newman smiled. "You don't know how much this means to me, to us. Patsy and I can go somewhere and start over. We won't have to stay here and battle things out."

Jesse squinted and started to sputter. He didn't know what to make of what Newman was saying. Grant could tell that he wanted to speak his mind, but his father thought better of it and just clenched his jowls tight under his whiskers. Jesse Grant, even silent, could be a figure of stern disapproval. Years of living with Hannah Grant had taught him well.

Grant could understand the thoughts, though. Newman would have a rough time keeping his secret in Bethel. Small towns didn't keep hidden lives. The townsfolk would know in a matter of months, and the trouble would begin. Grant had heard of secret organizations springing up in the South that lynched blacks who even looked at a white person. A full-fledged relationship was trouble brewing. Yet Grant also knew that money could grease enough wheels to make life easier for the both of them. Cash seemed to break down even the strongest of barriers and buffer the rich.

"So I'm assuming that you agree to these conditions?" Grant stood up and stretched. The day's activities and the long hours of sitting and explaining how they came to be in an abandoned root cellar had taken their toll on him. He was used to being more active.

Newman stood too, reminding Grant with his sticks that he'd helped save his family in the cellar. "Deal by me." Instead of offering Grant his hand, Newman held out a package of leather-bound notebooks.

Grant took the package with some shock. He hoped that Newman wasn't bribing him with a cut of the treasury for not telling the government. He would be mightily offended and consider changing his mind about the deal. The notebooks were held together with a piece of gray ribbon. Grant untied the knot and let the ribbon fall to the floor. He opened the first book and nearly choked on his tongue. He was holding the lost journals of Jefferson Davis.

Grant leafed through the pages of the first book. The Confederates would want these journals almost as much as they did the gold. Rumors had abounded that Jeff Davis wasn't in his right mind during those last bleak days of March and April. Anyone who thought his government could continue to function as it moved in railcars from city to city was a few bullets shy of a full revolver. Davis's attitude had been one of fighting for the cause at all costs, till the last man fell. He'd wanted to abandon the East and continue a guerrilla war from Texas. The loss of life would have been tremendous, and the war would still be puttering on. Most of the men who opposed this view resigned from the government rather than continue to fight with the strong president.

Even so, his arrest had sparked a furor both in the South and abroad. He'd been near walking dead when they arrested him. Just a man with a few troops left to protect him. The melancholia had set in on him as bad as it ever had for Lincoln. Davis's darkest moods had begun to lift during the four months he'd spent in prison, but people still clamored for his release on humanitarian grounds. If these notebooks could prove that Davis had gone around the bend, the legitimacy of the Confederacy would be dealt another blow. Nobody wants to think his own cause led by a mad man.

At first glance, Grant could find no signs of insanity in the writing, but he wasn't qualified to judge the man's soundness of mind. He would leave that to others. Davis's prose was clear, but not straightforward and precise like Grant's. The general had earned a reputation for his writing that had served him well in the Army. Soldiers would become confused with vague orders. Clarity of writing made that less likely. Still, Jefferson Davis had recounted without outlandish detail the final days of his administration, the only American president not representing the entire nation to ever exist. The books needed to be preserved.

Grant decided to put them away for another time when he could study them at his leisure. Most likely, the details would tell him about the former president's state of mind. He tried to imagine what Andy Johnson would say about retrieving the journals, which had been given up for lost when the troops who arrested Davis couldn't locate the books. Their disappearance only led credence to the claims that their contents needed to be hidden from the Federals.

As Grant started to head upstairs to see Julia, Jesse started asking Newman about receiving a commission for setting up the deal.

CHAPTER · 20

THROUGHOUT THE NIGHT, Grant could not sleep. As he tossed and turned, he decided to stroll the streets of Bethel at the cock's crow. He wanted the time to clear his head, and early morn was always best for that. He still wasn't satisfied with Mrs. Brown's guilt in the murders. She had confessed to the assaults and to trying to steal the map from their room at Newman's house. But she had steadfastly denied any part in killing Woerner or Halley, and that denial kept Grant from sleep.

He knew that he couldn't leave town until the matter was properly resolved. Yet his schedule was tight. Julia would be pushing him to move on soon and head towards Cincinnati, where the receptions would be more to her liking. Galas, speeches, and cheering crowds. Grant enjoyed the attention and the recognition of his success, but he dreaded the milling, teeming people who would be there.

Bethel, where the citizens could be counted in hundreds, was more comfortable to a simple man. Yet even here, everyone expected a certain behavior now that he had found success. He had become a man who clamored after accolades in their eyes, a famous man and not one of them.

The sun peered through the windows, and Grant rose, careful not to wake his wife and son. He strolled the streets with no apparent intent, but in a few minutes, he passed by Woerner's house. He thought that perhaps the answers he needed were inside. It was a long shot, but maybe he would find something that would give him the solution he wanted.

Grant craved certainty now that the war was over. All the hard decisions lay ahead for the nation. War had been straightforward compared to the impending political battles of Reconstruction. He wanted to face Washington with a clear conscience on the matter of the Confederate gold. He took the long front walk to the porch, opened the unlocked door, and went inside.

The smell of neglect had already begun to set in. It wouldn't take long in the damp, musty days of fall for rot and decay to take over. He'd seen it all over the South.

He started with the staircase again. It seemed a logical place to look, as Woerner had spent his last few moments alive there. Grant walked up and down the steps but found no signs of tampering other than what he'd seen before. He descended the stairs and noticed a long white thread on the bottom step.

He stooped to pick it up. The strand looked like a piece from a linen cloth. Or from someone who did tatting. Grant knew of only one person associated with the deaths who did that kind of work. He took a long deep breath and tried to think.

He wasn't sure how to approach the additional evidence any more than he was certain how to deal with the gold. Life held so many gray decisions where nothing was black and white, right or wrong. He could handle the situation in so many ways. In the war, he had pushed ahead, no matter what the cost in lives or bloodshed. Grant just didn't think of defeat, and, therefore, it didn't happen. He just thrust until he found a weak spot in the enemy to exploit.

He thought that would be the most practical approach in

this matter too, but he wanted a second opinion. His family would rule based on their own purposes: Jesse would consider the money, and Julia would want the most expeditious route.

Grant looked out the front window and saw the steeple of the Methodist Episcopal church. Perhaps the preacher would have a less biased opinion of the situation. Evans also knew the suspects and was likely to know more of what the ethical solution might be.

Grant strode over to the church, never breaking his fast pace. There would be none of the social chitchat or donations now. He was not his father in many ways. Grant had questions to be answered. These crimes had their roots deep in the personalities of the men he grew up with and their women. He wanted to know what Evans knew about the townsfolk—and how that knowledge might relate to the crimes. The preacher knew the changes in the town since the war. He also seemed to know how to make a dollar off those changes, and, Grant suspected, he had used his position to make a profit for his church.

The doors to the chapel were open. Grant stepped into the narthex and found Evans holding a large stack of gold coins. The man looked up, wearing an expression of raw lust on his face. His eyes were the size of the coins. The glazed look amazed Grant; it was as if the man had a glimpse of heaven.

Evans stood there for a second before he regained his composure, becoming the meek pastor once more. "General Grant, what an unexpected pleasure. What brings you back to our church? Your mother was a big supporter of ours, but I certainly can't compare anyone to our Clarissa Halley. She brought over another sizable donation."

"When did this happen?" Grant looked at all the gold and tried to calculate the amount. He didn't have his father's flare for money, but that was not a new thing. He'd had his financial failures rubbed in his face for too long to forget it. He wished he knew how much Newman had parceled out to the widow, but even without an accurate number, he was pretty sure that Mrs. Halley's entire portion lay before him on the floor of the church.

"She brought it over last night. She'd received a windfall from her family and wanted to share it with us. The Lord is at work."

Grant didn't relish the thought of a non-Sunday sermon. He'd heard enough of that on the weekends without adding to it now. Especially from Reverend Evans, who had shown his true colors when he thought he was alone. The greedy man who was planning his next building campaign should stumble over words about how the Lord worked.

Grant wondered how much pressure the preacher had put on the widow to make a contribution. Had he resorted to blackmail to get his hands on the money? Grant wasn't sure why someone would turn over the entire parcel without a fight. "Indeed He is, Reverend. Sometimes, we just don't know what ways the Lord works."

Evans nodded. "How true. I didn't know that Clarissa had any rich kin, and yet she's made two sizable donations to the church. I don't know what we'd do without her."

Grant nodded. "How much did she give?"

Evans smiled and motioned for Grant to follow him to the back of the church. "We can't discuss the specifics of another member of the congregation's giving, but the sum is over one thousand dollars. I simply can't believe it."

"Did she indicate why she did that? From my understanding, that was the entire sum she received from her inheritance. It's not a tithe. And with her husband dead, I would think that she would need all the money she could get for security."

Evans paused a moment, as if to think about the ramifications of taking the woman's last dollar. Grant wondered if the preacher had shaken her down for it and perhaps needed to reread the verses about the widow's mite.

"Well, to be honest," the minister explained, "she indicated that she didn't want the money. She didn't give me specifics, but apparently the source of the cash was distasteful to her. Giving it to the church was her way of doing penance for it. Making amends with her Maker."

Evans seemed to believe that money could be purified like a soul, merely by giving it to someone who wanted it as much as anyone else. He had plans for it, just like the Browns had, and just like the Confederate government had.

"Can that be done? Can you buy forgiveness?"

The preacher's lips pressed into a thin white line. "She's not buying forgiveness. She's making amends."

"To who? Her children won't have a comfortable life. She'll have to work or find someone to support her."

"She's going to live with relatives in Maysville next week. They've kindly agreed to take her in. She'll be selling the house, and she indicated that she'd have enough to live on from that."

Grant knew Maysville, a little town on the Kentucky side of the Ohio River, just across the water from Ripley. Many Ohio residents had come from Maysville, a popular crossing point of the river. Jobs were a bit easier to find in Southern Ohio, where industry had started to take root. The quiet, private ways of the people traveled across the river with them, though.

Kentuckians had not been as badly touched as the rest of the South. The border states had been problematic throughout the conflict. Most of Northern Kentucky had been protected from battle during the war because of its proximity to Ohio and the North. Even Jesse and Hannah Grant called Covington, Kentucky, home now. The most intense fighting had occurred south of the Mason-Dixon line. As such, most of Ohio didn't consider Kentucky to be the enemy, as they did Virginia and Georgia and other states where heavy battles had taken place.

Kentucky would never have been allowed to secede. Lincoln could not have stood for his home state to go with the Rebels and lose another free state in those first dire days of the war. Even so, Kentucky provided as many soldiers for the South as it did for the North. For every Lincoln, there was a Breckinridge, who had once been Vice President of the U.S. and had offered his services to the C.S.A.

Fortunately for the Union, the South had made an error in sending troops to Kentucky early on. That gave Lincoln sufficient reason to protect the state from the aggressors and install troops there. Those troops never left until Appomattox.

Yet for most Bethelites, Maysville might as well be the Oregon Territory. It was out of sight and out of mind of the people who had to focus on today for their existence. "What about her children? Won't they need to be protected and cared for?"

"God protects all of his own, General. Just as he watches the lilies in the valley, he watches over us. Clarissa will be well provided for by the Lord."

"And just what will her money be used for here? Feeding the poor? Rebuilding from the War?" Grant strolled up to the parson's desk and looked at the papers without disturbing them. He'd learned the old trick of reading upside-down memos during his years in the Army. The papers mostly dealt with the plans for an added wing to the church, a separate space for the choir, and a large new office for the pastor. Words like *mahogany* and *Italian marble* shot off the page at him. Grant doubted that Evans would know what God wanted from the money.

"We have a number of missions here in Bethel that will benefit from this munificence. The entire landscape of the town will be changed."

Grant sighed. He could tell that he wouldn't get very far with Evans. The money had started to leech out of the original group into society, causing havoc wherever it went. Grant winced at the thought. He could fight a war over political philosophy, or the concept of a strong Federal government, or even to free the slaves of the country, but he couldn't stand the notion of fighting a war to fill the coffers of a few. The idea sickened him in a way that few others did. He couldn't bear to think of the bodies rotting in Cold Harbor for the want of the almighty greenback.

Even Grant's own foibles during the war came from money. He'd received much grief for having issued a proclamation in the South, barring Jews from profiteering during the war. Black marketeers had made a fortune off of Southern cotton, which in turn bought guns and ammunition to shoot Grant's soldiers. The merchants indirectly aided the South in continuing their fight against the Union. Few people had known that Jesse Grant's partners in the illegal cotton trade were Jewish, and the order effectively threw his father out of the war zone. Grant had taken care of a family problem with a racist edict. He knew that, but he had to protect his own reputation. By the time he rescinded the decree, Jesse had been well schooled in what he could not do in trade.

Grant had been chastised for his anti-Semitic behavior, but it had found a better home in him than the fact that his father had made Greeley's headlines with stories of Jesse's shady methods of making a dollar. Grant's father had even had the nerve to write to Stanton requesting that the Department of War buy saddles from his store. By then, the general and Stanton knew each other well enough that the suggestion didn't harm their working roles.

Yet here stood a man of God, a man of the cloth, and he was just as tempted as any of the black-market bandits who had made Grant's life a misery during the war. Was this to be the way of the world after the war?

Grant made up his mind and took the back exit from the church. Though not as he intended, Grant knew what had to be done now.

Chapter · 21

HE'D NO SOONER GOT TO THE HALLEY PLACE than the door opened. Grant had come straight from the church, not wanting to waste more time. He and Julia wanted to continue their trip, and he didn't want the killer to slip through his fingers before he could stop the gold lust.

"I've been expecting you."

Grant didn't know how that could be; he'd only come to his conclusions a few minutes earlier. He looked at Mrs. Halley with his brows furrowed.

"You might as well come in." She held the door for him and let him pass. "Don't want all the neighbors to hear this. Or maybe they should."

Grant recalled the day of Halley's funeral and how crowded the house had been. Now there was only the rhythmic clack of a grandfather clock.

"Then you know why I'm here?" He was still puzzled by the woman's words. Certainly she couldn't have any intuitive powers so great to know his mind.

"You want me to confess to killing my husband and Adam Woerner."

Grant's eyes widened. He had been expecting a long discussion, leading up to the accusations. Here she had come out with it before they'd even gotten comfortable in their chairs. "Um, well, yes, I guess I would like that."

"Very well. Is there something you need me to sign? Or should I tell Crosson or a judge?"

Grant's chin about got splinters from hitting the floor. "A signed confession would be sufficient, I guess."

"Hmm, very well." The woman went to the next room and returned quickly with a sheet of paper and a fountain pen. She tapped the nib into the ink well and started to write. "Is there anything in particular that you wanted to know?"

Grant suspected a prank. No one could be this ready to incriminate herself for two murders. It wasn't right. His children denied taking sweets with less equanimity than this woman admitted to taking two human lives. Lee had put up more struggle in his surrender of a nation than this woman fought for her life. "How did you know that I was coming?"

She looked up from the paper for a second, and Grant at last caught a hint of emotion in her eyes. "That cursed Harriet Brown. She brought too much notice to the matter."

"How so?" Grant couldn't understand how a woman who almost took the blame for the crimes could have botched someone else's attempts to get away with the killings.

Mrs. Halley took a deep breath and let out a long sigh. "I certainly don't have to explain your thought processes to you, do I?"

Grant could barely explain them to himself, much less someone else. He suspected that one person couldn't be both the planned killer and the brash, money-hungry bumbler. He did know that the theft was bungled, as was the attempt on Newman's life with the rifle. Mrs. Halley's crimes were perfectly executed. Perhaps she was right that the brazen nature of Mrs. Brown had brought an unwelcome attention to the other deaths.

"So why did you tell us that you suspected your husband had been murdered? Why bring attention to your own crimes like that?"

Mrs. Halley took the time to dip her pen into the inkwell again and write another line before answering. "Isn't that obvious? People had begun to talk. You spoke with the doctor. Even though he and the coroner called it natural causes, these stupid people wanted to attribute it to me. You know that several people had mentioned the killing to Dr. Peck. I'd heard rumors of an exhumation. If I made the same claims about the suspicions, then I looked less guilty. Otherwise, I was the one who cooked my husband dinner and served him poisoned foods."

Grant nodded. Once a rumor was started, it took on a life of its own. Major Rawlins took great pains to battle the constant prattle of Grant's drinking problem, but the rumors were a Hydra that could never be vanquished. Every time that someone didn't like one of Grant's decisions, it was blamed on hooch. "So it was poison?"

She nodded as she continued to write. "Definitely. I had some arsenic left from some wasps I destroyed. It just took a bit in his food to do him in."

"And Woerner?"

"Adam Woerner got no better than he deserved. That man tried to coerce me into having knowledge of him in return for his silence. He'd noticed the arsenic missing from the root cellar. He'd gone in there to look at moving the money to our land and saw that the poison wasn't where it had been. Then he knew what had happened. I tried to offer him money, but he said that he had more than plenty of that. He wanted flesh." Her hands trembled slightly as she spoke.

Grant was glad to finally see some emotion out of her. The woman had seemed too in control of the situation, based on the most likely outcomes. He didn't think that Woerner had shown exemplary logic when he decided to blackmail a murderer. It's like sleeping with a cottonmouth. "So you tied a piece of linen across the top of the stairs and let him fall to his death."

She smiled. "That's right. After his latest demands, I determined to be quit of him. I took a piece of linen from Harriet's collection and tied it across the stairs. I've never been as glad to hear news of someone's passing as I was his. Then I went back later to put a linen thread on the steps. Harriet had become a thorn in my side."

Grant looked at her, but she seemed not to take in the gravity of what she'd done. She'd murdered two veterans without losing her composure. "The thread was a mistake," he said. "There had been half a dozen men in that room, looking for something to tie the crime to someone. We didn't find a thing that day, but two days later, a piece of string is there that points to one person only. Impossible."

She paused to think. "Perhaps you're right. But she had become a nuisance with all her shooting up town and such."

"Well, you were the most likely person to be in contact with linen thread after Mrs. Brown. So that made me start to consider you more seriously as a suspect."

She put the pen back to the page and continued writing. Her tongue stuck out of the corner of her mouth as she formed words. "Be that as it may, she used her gun to lay waste to my carefully made plans. So I tried to blame her for the deeds."

Grant watched the woman, but she seemed to make no attempt to leave or attack. She was content to sit at the desk and write out a confession. "So you're saying that she's the one who tried to kill Newman? Not you."

"Of course, she did. There was no finesse in shooting out someone's living room window. None at all. No one had connected me with Chris's death. It was considered to be accident or illness. Until she came along."

"Then people started to consider the possibility that all three men had been murdered. Young, Halley, and Woerner."

"She started those rumors as well. The maid to Mrs. Bly told me as much. She wanted the money for herself and wanted to see me hang for her crimes."

Grant watched the woman's eyes blaze as she spoke about her nemesis. Mrs. Brown didn't know how close she had come to facing a similar fate that the Union soldiers had at the hands of Mrs. Halley. "But you didn't do it for the money, did you?"

She punched the nib of her pen onto the paper and clenched her teeth. "Of course not. Though I doubt anyone will believe me. They'll think I wanted more for myself. They always think that men want more money."

"Money is the root of all evil." Grant knew the quote. His mother had repeated it so many times to him, though his father treated him as a failure for not making it.

Mrs. Halley gave him a smile that never even attempted to reach her eyes. The blue orbs were as cold as an ice floe on the Ohio River. "Actually, General, it's the *love* of money that is the root of all evil. Christopher was a changed man when he came back to Bethel. The money did that to him. The prison camp might have made him humble, but the money made him hard. He wanted to show everyone that he was a success. We had to move into this . . . monstrosity. We bought furniture—possessions. It consumed him, the feeling that he had to be better than the people here—our friends and our family. He began to see people as possessions as well, things that could be controlled with a carrot and stick of gold."

Grant nodded and thought of all the times that his father had tried to make him dance with his money, even going so far as to suggest that Julia and the children stay with Jesse and Hannah in Kentucky while Grant worked in Illinois. He had turned down that less-than-magnanimous offer. "You can't kill people."

"I know that it's wrong, but I feel the Lord would understand and provide for my family. It's not like I took a gun to them and shot them face-to-face. I wasn't even present when they met their Maker. Theirs were peaceful deaths. It was almost artistic."

Grant thought that the deaths might have been peaceful for the widow, but he doubted that Halley and Woerner would agree with that assessment. They were dead, no matter what the cause of termination.

"I couldn't bear the thought of living the rest of my life under the stigma of that money. I wanted to give it to the Lord to redeem myself."

"So you knew about the tontine? And the fact that if your husband died, the money would go to someone else? You'd get nothing."

Mrs. Halley signed her name to the document with a flourish and blotted the ink. "Of course. I wanted none of that money. The Rebs killed two of my brothers at Antietam. Their gold could not make that up to me. Money will never replace love and family. Don't you know that?" She handed him her confession.

Grant was shocked by how open and frank she was being with him. He accepted the paper and folded it. He slid it into the pocket of his worn overcoat, which he hadn't even bothered to take off since coming in. "So by killing your husband, you got away from the gold."

"Yes, I did. Or at least I thought I did. But Zeke Newman insisted on making a gift of more of it to me. I didn't want that. I didn't ask for it, so I gave it to the church. It could do good there. Perhaps that money would save someone's soul. Mine was redeemed there."

"Reverend Evans will be adding more rooms to the church

with all that money. Besides, you killed again after your husband."

"Adam Woerner died because he insisted on knowing me."

Grant nodded. "People didn't think that. They thought that Zeke Newman or Micah Brown were killing people to get more money."

"That's where Harriet Brown got her idea. Once it was down to two people, why not kill the other and take the entire fortune?"

Grant looked around the room. For someone who hadn't wanted material possessions, she'd done well for herself. It was all clear to him now. Mrs. Brown had capitalized on Mrs. Halley's crimes for her own ends. Unfortunately, the tatting housewife was not as methodical in her means as the widow. He was still contemplating the murders of the men he had known, when he looked up and saw the woman pull a Derringer from the bustle of her dress.

Grant was shocked. He never considered that she might have a weapon concealed on her person. But in women's fashions, a bustled dress and petticoats could hide an entire regiment and their arms.

He didn't pause to reflect any further. As she pulled out the weapon, he dove behind the sofa and scrambled to look for a means to protect himself. The room seemed to be cluttered in china and porcelain, but nothing seemed suited to defend himself from gunfire.

No wonder she had been so frank. She had no intention of letting him get out of the room alive. She could sign any number of papers and confessions, because she would take them back after she had slaughtered him like the others. He cursed his stupidity. No other soul knew where he was.

Grant waited for the sound of her dress as it shuffled on the floor. While her garments might make an ideal hiding place for armaments, they made for terrible gear for silent maneuvers. The rustle of her petticoats and stiff dress fabric would at least alert him to her movements.

He didn't hear the sound of anything for nearly a minute. The time passed as hours, each second a lifetime. His body reacted as it had in battle so many times. His hearing became sharp enough to hear the sounds of cattle lowing outside and the scream of a child in the distance. Each noise made his muscles clench tighter.

Still, she had to make some sound. It was impossible to move without it. Grant studied the terrain of the room while he waited. The door was about ten feet to his left. He could probably make it outside without being hit, if two chairs hadn't been in the way. He didn't know how he could move faster than her aim and still stay upright through the obstacles. Much as he hated to admit it, he was trapped in a well-decorated coffin with the woman.

He continued to wait. The tension was almost unbearable. He kept expecting the click of the trigger and the whiz of a bullet through the horsehair and fabric that made up his only armor. Not much consolation. His would not be an artistic death, though. Blood and body tissue would be hard to disguise from visitors. Unless she closed up the house before she had any more guests. Grant remembered that she was going to Maysville later in thc wcck. It might be months before someone noticed that the house carried dark stains on the floor and walls.

Julia, of course, would miss him immediately. She was expecting to leave for Cincinnati the next day. She would put out a call for him and would contact the sheriff about his disappearance. The one nice thing about celebrity was that it meant people were willing to expend resources to accommodate you. Grant expected the entire town would be out searching for him, but it would be too late for assistance.

He heard the unmistakable clack of the trigger, the first sound he'd heard come from the woman's direction. She must be planning a move, he thought. But he heard no rustle of fabric.

Suddenly the gun roared, and Grant flattened himself on the hardwood floor, waiting for the puncture of a bullet through his flesh. At this range, she would be hard-pressed to miss him. Still, after a few seconds, he felt no pain. The roar of the gun rang in his ears, and the thick acrid smoke filled his nose.

He debated that he was in shock and incapable of pain, but he couldn't see any rising red stains on his clothing. Had she missed him at such close range? Perhaps she was unskilled in arms.

The sounds and smells brought him back to the battles of the war. Had it been only six months? He felt like it had been forever, except for the parades. Had he survived all that, just to be felled by a woman who didn't want her share of a fortune? He hoped not.

Grant climbed up to a crouching position and looked over the sofa. Clarissa Halley hadn't missed her target. A dark patch on the wall had begun to trickle down the plaster, running red rivulets. What remained of her body was on the floor, gun still in her hand.

CHAPTER · 22

JULIA STEPPED UP into the carriage and settled herself in. The daily stage to Cincinnati was about to leave, and the family had all decided to go together. Grant wasn't sure about the thirty-some miles to Cincinnati with his father and his son vying for conversational supremacy, but he didn't have a choice in the matter.

Newman and Patsy had come out to see them off. At 5:00 A.M., when the "Night Hawk" was loading its passengers, the street was nearly deserted. Grant was glad for the quiet and peaceful country sounds, a natural lullaby that he wouldn't hear in Washington or even Cincinnati. He would be in big cities for some time to come.

The driver stowed the last of the luggage on board and hopped up to his station. Jesse climbed aboard and sat across from Julia. Little Jess took the seat next to his grandfather.

Grant gave a long last look to the town. He wasn't sure when he would be back through again. He couldn't know what the next few years would bring in terms of his ever-increasing busy schedule. The presidency looked more and more likely as his next occupation and the White House as his next home.

He shook Newman's hand and gave Patsy a peck on the cheek,

as he would the wife of any friend. At this hour, he could afford to be more generous with Newman's choice of companion.

"Thanks, Sam. I appreciate what you've done for us." Newman smiled and gave a nod of his head towards Patsy.

Grant mumbled a few words. He would be expected to give speeches and shake more hands in Cincinnati, and he dreaded the thought of all the politicking, though he enjoyed the accolades of the crowd.

He still hadn't truly recovered from the shock of Clarissa Halley's death. He wasn't sure what he'd expected to happen. She would have been arrested and tried for the murders, but so few juries believed that a woman, who couldn't vote or do so many things, could be capable of committing any number of hideous crimes. The same fair sex that brought life into the world could remove it just as easily.

Still, he hadn't expected her to take her own life in front of him. For a woman who had preached to him about greed and salvation, she had surprised him by committing suicide.

The church was having problems deciding what to do with the most generous donor in their congregation. The money she had given was balancing the scales of justice with her crimes and sins. Grant was sure that Evans would find a way to slip Mrs. Halley into the cemetery in some manner.

Her children were going off to Maysville to stay with relatives, and Evans had promised to check in with them from time to time to make sure that nothing was wanted. The sale of the house and contents would provide them with enough money to get a good start in life.

Newman had offered assistance to the family beyond that. With all that money and the padding against life that it afford him, he could be generous. And the man knew what it was like to be an outcast in society. Perhaps he and Patsy could help them with comfort as well as cash.

Grant was glad to know that the children of his fighting friend would be well taken care of. He was still able to feel some compassion for them, even after the crimes Halley's wife had committed. He knew that a child wasn't responsible for the sins of the parents. He was living proof of that. But in a small town like Bethel, they would always be known as children of a killer.

Grant climbed into the carriage and closed the door. He leaned back in the seat and settled in for the long ride to the next town.

ALSO BY JEFFREY MARKS

The Ambush of My Name

Ulysses Grant returns to Georgetown, Ohio, after the Civil War, expecting parades and praise. Instead he finds the body of a man in his hotel room, and the evidence points to a connection with Lincoln's assassination. The reappearance of his childhood sweetheart only complicates matters. Delving into the town's secrets, Grant realizes that not everyone wishes him well in the upcoming presidential election. With the help of a Pinkerton agent and an ambitious reporter, Grant has to discover who wants to turn a triumphant homecoming into a deadly trap.

". . . a tasty little mystery . . . . [Marks] juggles suspects as expertly as a circus performer, right up to the last chapter."

—*The Cincinnati Enquirer*

"In general, and with no pun intended, *The Ambush of My Name* is an interesting and entertaining addition to the growing number of Civil War mystery novels."

—*Civil War Book Review*

"Jeffrey Marks has achieved what every writer hopes to do; he's penned a novel that grabs the reader on the first page and doesn't let go."

—Cameron Judd, historian and Civil War author.

"Jeffrey Marks illuminates the forgotten years of Ulysses S. Grant in a debut novel full of intriguing history, appealing characters, and a very clever, climactic twist."

—Mark Graham, Edgar-nominated author of
the Wilton McCleary series of Old Philadelphia

"It's a fascinating story, with both suspense and humor and a most surprising ending."

—Sharan Newman, author of the critically acclaimed
Catherine LeVendeur medieval mystery series

Hardcover ISBN 1-57072-184-X $23.95
Trade Paper ISBN 1-57072-185-8 $13.95

ANTHOLOGY BY JEFFREY MARKS

Magnolias and Mayhem

Several of today's top Southern mystery writers spin yarns of murder and mischief south of the Mason-Dixon line: Jeff Abbott, Deborah Adams, Noreen Ayers with A. B. Robinson, Carolyn G. Hart, Beverly Taylor Herald, Dean James, Andrew Kantor, Toni L. P. Kelner, Jeffrey Marks, Margaret Maron, Taylor McCafferty, Elaine Fowler Palencia, and Elizabeth Daniels Squire.

— *Magnolias and Mayhem is a 2001 Anthony nominee* —

"Take your mint julep out to the veranda, then get ready for murder and moonlight—tempered with soft Southern charm."

—*Meritorious Mysteries*

"Bravo to this eclectic group of authors digging deep into the heart of the South. Their stories are rich in suspense, humor, and charm."

—Sujata Massey

"From urban Louisville, Kentucky, to the beach resort of Wilmington, North Carolina, and back in time to the Battle of Vicksburg, the authors render a South rich in Place; teeming with characters both quirky and complex; and punctuated with dialogues whose rhythms make me want to dance in praise."

—Anne Underwood Grant,
author of the Sydney Teague series

"Each story provides a full picture of the area to include powerful characterizations and many amusing scenarios. . . . Fans of the Southern crime story will fully enjoy this anthology intended for leisure reading over several cold nights."

—*The Midwest Book Review*

Hardcover ISBN 1-57072-112-2 $24.50
Trade Paper ISBN 1-57072-128-9 $15.00

www.jeffreymarks.com